Old Flames
Burn Manvi

MICHAEL ANDRE-DRIUSSI

"Among the Shattered and Debris" was first published in *Bards and Sages Quarterly*, January 2013.

"A Breen Carnation" was first published in *OG's Speculative Fiction Magazine #33*, November 2011.

"Daughter of Plant and Woman" was first published in *Twisted Fairy Tales, Vol. II*, 2011.

"Generation Cleansing" was first published in *M-Brane SF #12*, January 2010.

"Hardboiled Proust" was first published in *M-Brane SF #20*, September 2010.

"Hitler's Hollywood" was first published in *Big Pulp Winter 2012*, December 2012.

"I, Mombot" was first published in *M-Brane SF #14*, March 2010.

"Junkboy and Debutante" was first published in *M-Brane SF #26*, March 2011.

"Mad Dogs of Mercury" was first published in *M-Brane SF #16*, May 2010.

"Mayhem at Manville" was first published in *Bastion*, November 2014.

"Old Flames in New Bottles" was first published in the *ParaSpheres* anthology, Omnidawn Press, 2006.

"The Tavern of the First Village" was first published in *Child of Words #1*, March 2014.

CONTENTS

OLD FLAMES IN NEW BOTTLES

Julie had not come home the night before, so it was really, finally over between us. I was pretty dark about the whole thing — especially since she was the one to leave — but it was a bright, beautiful, Sunday morning in autumn, making up for a cold and dreary Bay Area summer. It was the perfect setting for a new beginning.

Cindy stroked my chin, saying "Chuck-chuck," her chin-stroking phrase. "Hey Mikey, don't be so down. She was no good for you. Too wooden, too plastic. Could she sing at all?"

"No," I admitted.

"There you go, then!" Cindy looked like a million bucks, like a young Angie Dickinson wearing a furry white coat over a clingy gray dress. She slipped her arm through mine as we walked up the rise of Solano Avenue, heading toward the Berkeley Hills — I caught a glimpse of us reflected in a shop window and God, we looked cute. Too bad she doesn't like men. Still, the perfect decoy.

We were trawling in a new area, a tiny town called Albany just north of Berkeley. It was about midway between my place and hers. Since Solano has a lot of restaurants, cafés, and wine bars, I'd somehow gotten the idea that there would be champagne brunches up and down the street every Sunday. That was my plan: we would cruise the brunches and winebars, looking for new lovers.

We walked and we walked but there were no brunches to be found. Nothing was open — the place was as dead as a blue-law town — and there were few people on display. My mood spiraled down like a nicked clay pigeon and my thirst increased. Up near the Berkeley border there was "Michael's Liquors," and it was open, so we went in and I bought a bottle of champagne and some cookies. Drinking on the sidewalk in front of a liquor store just seemed too depressing to contemplate, so we walked a couple more blocks and found a sunken little park with several benches and only one sleeping homeless guy.

After we sat down and took a few swigs, Cindy said, "So, where'd she go?"

"Up in the hills, probably," I said. "She's housesitting a mansion up there. Now she's with that black guy, Joe." I drank. "Damn, it's my fault, too. I actually said to her, 'You have to choose between us.'"

"Oh, no."

"Can you believe it? I must've been possessed or something."

"So who is this Joe?"

"What, I didn't tell you? I haven't even talked to you in months?"

"You've been too happy," she said.

"Maybe," I scoffed, biting into a cookie. "The guy is a freak — I mean really, a circus freak."

"Ouch!"

"No, he's not freakish-looking — he looks pretty normal, in fact. He just has this weird power, or a gimmick, probably — he makes things burn. Like spontaneous combustion."

"With his hands?" She had her skeptical look, watching for a joke.

"It seems like it's his breath."

"You're kidding," she said. I shook my head. "Okay, where'd you see him do this? On a stage?"

"No, out in the open," I said. "Down by the bay there's this landfill with a bunch of homeless people camping out. You know the kind of weird outdoor art galleries that pop up by the water? Things made with odd bits of junk, paintings on pieces of scrap wood? There's one over there. It's like a seedy little carnival, and it attracts weird little sideshows from all around.

"So this guy Joe, he's from Michigan. Joe Blowtorch or just Joe Blow. He took out a candle from this bag, and he blew it so it lit. He got out a newspaper and held it up, reading by the candle light, but when he got to the funnies he laughed and the paper burst into flames."

"Stage stuff," said Cindy. "So he's a performance artist. Julie's drawn to that, right? Since you met her when we were singing on Telegraph."

Telegraph Avenue was our trawling ground before: I'd play my acoustic guitar, looking like Donovan with a Lou Reed attitude, and Cindy would sing into a hair brush. We were just another sidewalk act, like the beggars, the runaways, the punks, the college students, and the tourists in that neighborhood. But we were sick of the scene there, the same faces and bodies. The familiarity that breeds contempt. In our last run Cindy got Kim and I got Julie, but we had fished that area out.

"She was a fan."

"Probably our only fan," said Cindy with a snort. "But those old torch songs were fun." And then she sang the title phrase of Peggy Lee's "Fever," that sultry song of sickness, love, and fire.

We left the half-empty bottle and the remaining cookies with the sleeping bum and walked further up the street. The sky was blue and clear except for a single billowing cloud to the southeast, a white column that rose from the Oakland hills. The cloud was smoke, and for an instant it hit me like a deeply private message broadcast across the city: Julie and Joe were having sex for all to see, and I was the one with the knife in his heart, I was the one filled with sadness at being left behind, I was the one flooded with burning jealousy. But then the internal and external worlds reversed themselves, and the smoke became an exclamation point for a disaster unfolding.

"Cindy, I've gotta go — it's Julie!"

"What?"

"I'll call you!" I bolted from Cindy's side, ran down the street. At the liquor store I heard the sound of a TV reporter talking about the fire, so I ducked in for a look: images of the conflagration flashed across the TV screen. The blaze had started only about a half-hour before but was already over a mile wide, sweeping down the hills with winds from the east. There was a shot of the stately white Claremont Hotel being evacuated with orange flames visible in the distance, an image that set me running again since Julie's mansion was up in that area.

A call to the mansion from a payphone gave me a busy signal. I made an emergency break-through but the operator said that there was nobody on the line, the phone was just off the hook.

I got to my car and sped toward the Claremont, avoiding the freeways because the fire had already engulfed the two over there. South of campus it was becoming overcast above and chaotic below, with sirens wailing around while gawkers lined one side of the road and fire refugees crammed the other. Turning up Dwight Way, onto Warring, I got lost in the maze of one-way streets and finally parked by a school. I got out and ran: it was quicker on foot.

The smoke was getting thicker, the hotel evacuation was still on — cars fleeing out of the parking lot and into the road chaos, burning embers drifting down. The news crews were filming everything, the barkers at a carnival show. I was swimming against the current, dodging cars and cutting through the hotel to get to the road behind it,

Alvarado, a winding street with pedestrian shortcuts. I ran up into that posh neighborhood of mansions and eucalyptus. It seemed everything was burning. I saw some people, crazy gawkers enjoying the carnival, maybe some looters, maybe a few crazy rescuers like me. I heard a popping sound a few times before I understood it was the sound of gas meters exploding in the heat — I heard another pop and looked over to see a new three-foot flame jetting from a house main.

The mansion Julie was housesitting was one of the few that was not on fire. I pounded on the door, shouting at the top of my lungs. It occurred to me then that she might not be there anymore, she might be somewhere else with Joe, that I was on a fool's errand. I smashed a window with an ornamental stone and then the door flew open.

"What are you *doing?*" she shouted, looking like Natalie Wood playing Veronica-with-a-hangover, clutching a bathrobe around her.

"The hill's on fire!" I yelled. "We have to get out!"

"It's just overcast," she said. "Why don't you just leave me alone?"

"Huh?!"

"I took the phone off the hook and ignored the door pounding before, but this time you're breaking things!"

"*This* time?" I said. "This is the first time, I didn't call you before! I mean, I called one time, and the line was busy." She was smirking. "Look, come here, right over here and look at the neighborhood. Don't you hear that roaring sound — you think *fog* makes noise like that?"

"You mean you hear that, too?" she said, the light dawning upon her brow. "I thought it was just my head."

I won her over to the fire situation but she still had to get dressed and find her purse. It seemed crazy to me, like she was stalling or something. As I helped her I tried to ignore the signs of Joe's recent presence there — the most glaring detail being the rumpled bed sheets which had been scorched. I swallowed my pride.

Finally we left and ran downhill, through areas of danger toward safety. We became giddy with relief as we came out into the normal world by the Claremont, and Julie pulled me into a long hot kiss like she'd never done before.

I wanted to find my car and take us home but she wanted a room, so we walked to the nearest motel and consummated our reunion. We were together again, our problems had vanished like smoke — where last week we had been treating each other like strangers, now it was hot and heavy again. I was the brave hero who had saved her, so when she told me to tie her down I did it with love instead of the resentment I'd felt in the past, and when I dripped the hot candle wax onto her I was not a puppet, I was her puppet. As well as the brave hero, who now fiddled while Rome burned.

After the third time she smiled languidly and said, "This seems like a new beginning."

"Yeah," I said, brushing the moxibustion incense ash off of her. I was sore and happy and sleepy.

"Let's make it real," she said. "Let's make a clean break with the past. Get rid of everything from before, make a fresh start."

"'Everything' like the apartment?" I said, my fingers fumbling stupidly at the knots that held her.

"'Everything' like the apartment and all the stuff inside it," she said. "Clothes, books, TV, everything."

"Huh," I said. "And how are we going to do this? I'm in between jobs and you don't have one, either."

"Well," she said, looking away and biting her lower lip, "the mansion belongs to my father."

"It does?"

"And we could stay there, rent free. Please, master?"

"If it doesn't burn down . . . ," I said, and she smiled.

I tried to call Cindy, to let her know that Julie and I were safe from the fire, but there was no answer. Not even her machine.

•

Miraculously the mansion did not burn down, and we moved in a few days later. Julie bought me new clothes and papers to sign for the apartment and the car. I kept trying to call Cindy and eventually got a guy who said there was no Cindy there. It was as though she had been disposed of along with all the stuff of my past life.

November was a time of clean up and rebuilding in the footprint of the fire. But not for us, the luckiest of the lucky ones: the mansion had a luxury sedan in the garage, and we took it for a week-long tour of the Gold Country, where the turning leaves were a blaze of color. I looked forward to meeting her father, who seemed to be always traveling. Julie told me he was in Texas then.

The weather in December grew cool and I learned through trial and error how to set a proper fire in the mansion's fireplace. (Obviously a single log does not burn, but I learned that even two logs with lots of kindling do not really burn. The minimum number is three.) The night we had a Yule log in there, burning away at the one end, as we sat on the sofa sipping wine, Julie turned to me and said, "I'm pregnant."

I was completely surprised, feeling several conflicting emotions in rapid sequence: betrayal, a sense of entrapment; joy at the prospect of having a child with the woman I loved; fear of the unknown; and the corrosive doubt as to whether the child was mine. The stage was set: there were many ways I could play this scene, but I knew in my heart the best way for the brave hero of my new life. I got down on both knees and said, "Will you marry me?"

She blinked back tears as she said, "You must not kneel, you must stand. Barefoot."

I was stunned, but I did as she said. She knelt and said to the floor, "Your wish is my command." Then she kissed my foot and wept.

We got married, a minimalist civil ceremony. As a wedding present her father, who was in Colorado at the time, sent a man and woman to help with the mansion: Frank, a Southerner with a pasty-white complexion, and Mrs. Limburgh, a rosy mountain of the kitchen.

Those were beautiful days of bright expectation. It was like we were two kids playing house. That winter brought storms that broke the five-year drought, a dry spell that had made the firestorm possible. There were times when it would rain and, through some trick of the light, it would seem like the rain was glowing — and I would open my mouth and catch some rain on my tongue, and it was sweet like honey with a hint of turpentine. It was like manna from heaven, it was so wonderful; yet I came to accept it as normal, just another manifestation of my new life.

Julie hired a midwife and a nanny, the first one a seasoned pro and the other a fresh college grad. We were six living in the mansion then, with me as a sort of gentleman gardener, always tending to the yard and doing home repair jobs. Julie's father was in Azerbaijan, then in the Philippines, then in Saudi Arabia. Julie said he would come to "Oaktown" for the birth of the baby. She called Oakland "Oaktown," and even though I'd never heard that name before, it seemed like everybody used it.

By April the rains had stopped and there was a new city ordinance for each household to do its own raking and burning of leaves in order to eliminate the danger of firestorm. So I did that, and after a bit of smoke and fire I started having sex with the nanny. Furtive sex at odd times of the day and night. Julie had swollen up, had metamorphosed into a new non-sexual creature nearly the size of Mrs. Limburgh, our cook, but I had not changed: I was still sexual and had never been aroused by the sight of a pregnant woman. I cannot excuse it. The pressures of waiting on a pregnancy are there, and the close company of a pretty, young, non-pregnant woman contributed. Whatever resistance I had was completely lost the first time, or so I thought.

This went on for a few months. Julie and her midwife would go off to some birthing class and we would couple like rabbits. No bondage, no props, just simple rutting.

It all ended one night in July when Frank the butler caught us going at it in the upstairs bathroom. It was like a splash of cold water had awakened me from an erotic dream. I was ashamed, my head racing with incredible lies I could tell him to somehow convince him that he had not seen what he had thought he had as I tried to disentangle myself. But she was laughing, an odd bleating kind of laugh tinged with scorn. She said, "You don't even know my name, do you?"

I did not, in fact, because we all called her "Nanny": one of our private jokes was that now we had been intimate I could call her by her first name, "The."

But I thought I knew her real name, that I had heard it in passing somewhere: it was "Pamela" or "Tamara." So I tried to say one or both at once, but the sound that came out of my mouth was only the background noise of a fire crackling in a fireplace, or the rush of air when a BART train goes by.

She was not impressed either way. But I was, because I remembered that Pamela and Tamara were two of my former girlfriends, and in my heightened state I saw that The somehow contained both of them, or the essences of what I had loved of them, like old flames in a new bottle. I had awakened from a living dream, one where I was a Ken doll in Barbie's dollhouse; a "sadistic" prince who was supplied with Skipper as an official concubine. But just as suddenly I knew that it was all created, maintained, and directed by Julie — we were all merely her puppets. Or worse: I was a fly caught in her web.

I put my clothes on and went downstairs in search of Frank, thinking on several different tracks all at once. Would he tell Julie, or perhaps worse, tell her father who was in Manhattan at that time? Would he tell no one? He was in the backyard, blowing smoke rings in the misty moonlight.

"Hello Frank," I said, trying to keep my voice steady.

"Good evening, sir."

"About that, in the bathroom — I don't know what you saw, but . . ."

"Saw, sir? I saw nothing." His hands were empty, his behavior bland and polite. So the secret was safe. Or was it? It would always be there to be used against me.

I felt the coils tightening around me. I could stay as a drone of the hive, I could even continue with adulterous affairs so long as they were discreet, but suddenly the whole thing seemed like a living death. My own biological nature was revealed to me, stark and plain: I was interested in insemination, even fulfilled by impregnation, but I was not made for parenting.

In a broken rush I confessed all of this and more to Frank, and he said, "While it is none of my business, sir, such is not uncommon." This made me feel better, since I was feeling like an aversion to parenting made me a sub-human monster.

"Self-knowledge is important, sir," he continued. "With that, one can make the choice."

"I have made the choice," I said, feeling a new elation. "I am going to leave right now. I am going to take her with me and get my old life back."

"Make the choice, sir, and don't look back."

I went back inside and found The in her room. When I told her my plan she balked. We heard the return of Julie and her midwife from one of their birthing activities. The was too ashamed to stay in the house if I left, but she was also too ashamed to be seen leaving with me.

"You go first," she said, her face flushed as if she had a fever. "Start the car in the garage. I'll creep in and hide on the back seat. Then you drive on out."

It seemed silly but I agreed. I went to the garage and started the car as the garage door was rising. Outside the mist had thickened into fog. The passenger door behind me opened, then I heard her crawl in and the door closed softly.

"All ready?" I asked.

"Yes," she said, her voice muffled. "Don't look back, just drive."

As I put it in gear I started singing Peggy Lee's "Fever" like it was a protective spell. We were moving down the driveway, moving past the front porch. The song of love-sickness came pouring out of me but it seemed less meta-phorical than before.

There was motion in the rearview mirror and I looked. I heard The's voice give a moan as I saw Julie standing on the porch, her arm draped around Frank who stood on a lower step. She looked as beautiful as the day I first met her. The moan changed into a sharp little cry that was cut off.

"Are you okay?" I asked, craning my neck to look in the back seat. There was something back there under a black cloth, something about the size of a basketball, but it clearly was not Nanny.

I stopped the car and got out. I heard a sound like the name I had spoken to The, but it was not fire crackling or rushing air after all, it was the natural sound that fog makes. The two on the porch were laughing, and it dawned on me that Julie was slim now and Frank was Joe in a disguise that he was shedding. I opened the car door and beneath the black cloth I found a glowing sphere. The moment I picked it up I was knocked backward, engulfed in flames. There was a fetid stench of unwashed bodies and halitosis, burnt hair cut through by the clean scent of burning pine and eucalyptus. I rolled over and over, cling-ing to the bundle, with something scratchy on my face and throat. I felt like I was back in last year's firestorm — the grass around me was burning and I saw no sign of the car or the mansion.

In my arms I found a dead infant so badly charred that her hands and feet were black skeletal twigs.

When I came back to consciousness a paramedic was asking me what month it was, and I said July. I looked around and saw we were somewhere in the Oakland hills where a grass fire had just been put out, so I said it was October. She asked me what year it was and I said 1992, or 1991. I was scratching at my face and neck, they felt sunburned, and it came to me that the furry pelt in the way was in fact a thick and tangled beard.

My clothes were filthy rags, my body a reeking mess.

She said, "We found you with a baby. Whose was she?"

"I don't know," I said. Then I started to weep. "She was mine."

"What do you mean, she was yours?" the paramedic snapped, as if I'd really said something crazy. "Where's the mother?"

"Back at the mansion, I guess . . ."

A blonde paramedic arrived, surveying the area before she said, "Hey Jessica, whatta we got?"

"Hey Cynthia," said my paramedic. "Just this one guy with burns and a D.B. Baby Doe."

"We're lucky this time," said Cynthia with a relieved grin.

"Cindy!" I said. "I tried to call you months ago but your number was changed."

She bristled. "Nobody calls me that name —" She did a double-take looking at me, and looking at her I had my own doubts: this woman was heavier than Cindy, and looked to be older, in her thirties at least.

"Hey, sorry —"

"Mikey? Mikey, it's you!" she said. "Where the hell have you been? Jess, I haven't seen this guy for ten years!"

"Oh, come on," I said, laughing. "More like ten months!"

Confusion crossed her face, clouding her happy features. "No Mikey," she said, shaking her head as a few tears fell. "It has been ten — eleven years since you disappeared." She hugged me and then held me at arm's length. "My God, what happened to you? How long have you been living on the street?"

"I haven't been living on the street," I said. "I've been living in a mansion."

"Dressed like *this?*"

"No," I said. "I don't know where these clothes came from."

•

They put me under psychiatric observation and evaluation. Since I had been found at the center of the grass fire, not at the edge, it does not seem I was running from a fire but carrying it with me. The preemie was burned far in excess of what one would expect from a simple grass fire, and yet I, who was carrying it, suffered only minor burns. Some thought I was an arsonist, others thought I had accidentally started the blaze with a hobo cook fire, and the most charitable thought I had just been caught in the fire and tried to save the baby. But there was no evidence of a campfire, no sign of incendiary devices, nothing of the kind: only a bottle of champagne, half full, and a partial box of cookies. I myself was just confused — I thought the fire was caused by the preemie's spontaneous combustion, which they could not believe, and I had somehow lost more than ten years, which they would not believe.

DNA testing confirmed that the preemie was my daughter. Some thought that her mother might have died in the fire but her remains were never found; others thought she had just run off in a different direction.

They took me to the address of Julie's mansion but the place there was completely different since the old place had burnt down back in '91. They could find no record of Julie, no record of our marriage, nothing.

So the only thing that seemed to fit the facts was that I had been caught up in the '91 fire, where I suffered a severe trauma and lived as an amnesia bum for eleven years until the grass fire of '02 "woke me up"; or I lived as a bum until the grass fire gave me delusions of grandeur that made me forget my life as a bum.

•

Cindy came to visit me, which made me happier than I can say. We sat in the dayroom and she told me about her life immediately after my disappearance. "I was like, numb for a few days or a week, but then it started to seem like it was a message for me, that I really should get into fire fighting like I'd been thinking of."

"Yeah, I remember," I said. "You were talking about police or fire, tired of being a secretary. I thought it was just talk, but yeah, one time you said that the hardest part you could imagine about fire would be . . . the dead kids." I thought of the preemie and felt sad.

"I think it is even harder when you have kids," she said. "Something happens where every kid you see is your kid."

"Wait," I said. "You have kids?"

"Huh-yeah," she said in boyish embarrassment that tore my heart open. "Me and my partner Lola. The big one is six, the little one is four."

I was groping for something to say, something positive. I had never thought of her as being a parent — my head filled with all the declarations made to me that she would not be a parent. We had been heartbreakers, the dynamic duo of debauchery, and now she was a settled mother of two.

She filled in by changing the subject a little. "So when you told me, you know, that part about how you felt excluded from, uh, Julie's pregnancy? I can totally relate to that since I felt the same way the first time." I felt a little better until she added, "But I didn't cheat on her."

"Well, uh, how did you handle it the second time?" I said.

"I had the second one."

My world was breaking up again and I was weeping. "I'm sorry Cindy, I'm just so messed up. I'm happy for you but I'm sorry for myself, and God, I guess I've really been crazy for ten years."

She put her forehead against mine and said, "Hang on, hang on. I'm gonna tell you something, but God, I could lose my job or something." She leaned back, took a breath. "It's about the day of the Oakland hills fire. You ran off to find Julie or whatever and I started walking back down the street. After a few blocks there was an empty lot on one corner, the slab of an old foundation with a cyclone fence around it. At first I thought I'd just missed seeing it before, but then I noticed it was kitty-corner to the Safeway super-market, and I remembered seeing the Safeway sign like that when we came out of the liquor store. But the store wasn't there anymore.

"I couldn't believe it at first, but I looked around and there was no other liquor store anywhere near there. I went over to Safeway and asked this worker who was collecting the shopping carts and she told me the place had burned down a few months before, that it looked like arson, and that it had been called Michael's Liquors.

"I was so freaked I thought I was going insane. And then you disappeared, which was bad enough by itself, but it also meant that there was nobody else who had seen it. And that's why it seemed like a message for me."

She leaned forward and said, "I believe your story."

"You do?"

"Look, you haven't aged ten years — your face looks the same, especially without that beard." She glanced around to make sure we were not being watched too closely. "I'm not sure exactly what happened, but you and me both went into a place that wasn't really there, came out with food and drink which we ate and drank, and then all sorts of weird stuff happened."

I felt a strange peace then, thinking that maybe I had not lost my mind, after all. This was a gift that Cindy had given me.

After a quiet moment, Cindy asked, "What would've happened, do you think, if you had not looked back?" I must have given her a blank look, since she continued. "You know, when you were driving out and you glanced at the rearview mirror?"

"I don't know," I said. "I can't imagine."

All I know is, I awoke to find myself alone on the burning hillside, and I kept repeating, *"What a lovely way to burn."*

GENERATION CLEANSING

Sixteen-year-old Venus d'Malibu had been behind walls for four years, so the sight of a public gallows shocked her. In the bright sunlight of L.A., eight girl scouts stood with nooses around their necks, the scene framed by towering palm trees. Three of the girls were Brownies, too light for a proper hanging, so the hazmat-hooded executioner was putting bricks into one's little backpack. The impatient crowd waiting on the plaza was made up of Pures in their twenties — all the men with facial hair and sunhats, all the women with solar veils and solar hoods.

Venus blurted out, "Granma, what —?"

"Say that again and I'll kill you myself!" hissed Helen, who, being a real old lady, could get pretty scary at the drop of a hat.

Now Venus understood why Helen and the other adults back at the place had made her go out disguised as an old lady. The tight corset that bent her back and made it impossible for her to draw a full breath, the grey-dyed hair, the binding on her knee that made the prop cane a necessity. It wasn't to avoid harassment or rape, as she had thought — it was to avoid execution.

Venus shivered. She pulled her hoodie down and push-

17

ed her sunglasses up.

It was springtime, 2057. Venus and Helen were trying to get into the Los Angeles maglev train station but the lynch mob had stopped them at the plaza.

"Mabuhay!" shouted Helen, her voice strong for an eighty-year-old. She pumped her fist in the air and shouted, "Gen Clen!"

Others took it up, chanting and gesturing.

"Come on," said Helen. She pulled Venus and went toward the gallows, moving through the narrow passageway that had opened up.

Venus saw a group of Pures in white lab coats standing up on the gallows, each holding a compact submachine gun. Then she noticed other white coats at the edge of the crowd.

Two rows from the platform, Venus suddenly recognized the girl on the end and stopped in her tracks.

"Himiko," she said. Back when Venus went to school, the girl had been her best friend, and now she stood up there, looking out across the plaza, tears coursing down her cheeks.

Himiko looked down, seeming to lock eyes with her just before Helen yanked her forward.

Venus tore her eyes away to look at the other girls. She didn't recognize the next one, but the third was Saffron, and next to her was Teal. The three were movie-brats, old friends she had partied with and fought with, trading jewelry and make-up and boys. They didn't look like urban guerrillas.

"What did they do?" she asked without thinking when they were blocked for a moment.

"This is payback," said a bearded stranger beside her. "Some feral boys killed a white coat."

Venus felt the vomit rising up her throat but suddenly the girls dropped through the trap doors and the crowd roared.

Helen pulled Venus through the last row and under the

gallows, releasing her only to grab at Himiko's kicking legs. Venus felt an intense rush of joy, supposing her grandmother was somehow going to help the girl escape. Venus moved to assist, but Helen yelled, "I got this one — pull the next," as she pulled down on the girl so that her kicking stopped.

Venus vomited then, hunched over on the pavement with death twitching above her. She was jostled and nearly trampled before Helen hustled her out, saying, "My sister gets overexcited." It took Venus a while to grasp that Helen was talking about her, making excuses to other people.

The crowd inside the station was older and much less militant. Most of the men were clean-shaven. There were long lines but only a few white coats around.

Once they were in line, Helen said, "Andrea, you lost your cane, you silly old bird."

"I'm sorry," said Venus, her voice trembling with fake age or real emotion.

"That's all right. You stay here and I'll go find it."

"No!" Venus clutched at her. "Don't leave me!"

"Don't be silly. You'll be fine. I'll be right back."

Venus first felt abandoned and exposed, then she felt her neck and ears burn as if everyone was staring at her. The nearest white coat shifted her stance, making Venus catch her breath. She forced herself to look ahead at nothing, mentally rehearsing her lines.

I was playing bingo at the Silverado.

A few minutes passed. A new window opened at the counter. The middle-aged man who had opened the cloth tape barrier walked up to Venus and offered his arm, showing her a traditional respect for the aged.

She didn't want to go to the new line but she didn't want to draw attention to herself, either.

"Thank you," she said in her new granny voice, a breathiness made easier by the corset.

Now she was third in line, with no sign of Helen. She

broke out in a cold sweat that sent an icy river down her back. She closed her eyes and practiced her lines.

She was second in line for a while, then first in line. Still no sign of Helen. Finally the moment came when the mustachioed man at the counter waved her over and said something as she shuffled to him.

"I was playing bingo at the Silverado," she said, leaning on the counter to steady herself.

The man blinked and tilted his head. "Ma'am?"

"I'm sorry," she mumbled. She saw with alarm he was in his 30s. Would he lean young or old? She needed him to lean old, to be traditional, but he looked like he leaned young, toward the Pure. "What were you saying?"

"Passport please, ma'am."

"Oh, oh. Of course." When she handed it to him she saw that her hand was quivering with fear. She felt certain she was about to be caught.

"Thank you ma'am," said the man. He flipped open the passport and said, "Please remove your sunglasses."

"My —? Oh, I didn't know I had them on! Dumb bunny."

As she took them off with shaking hands she looked over her shoulder, searching for Helen and avoiding eye contact.

"You seem distracted, ma'am."

"What? Oh, yeah. My little sister went back out there — I left the cane somewhere. Nope, I still don't see her."

Steeling herself, she turned and looked him straight in the eye. He nodded and glanced at the open passport.

"Please tell me your decanting date."

"I was *born*," she lied, "and I'll bet you were, too. Nothing to be ashamed of."

"The date?" he asked, like he'd heard it all before.

"Four-five-six-seven," she said in a sing-song way. "I'll be a hundred before you know it."

"Where were you on VC Day?"

"I was playing bingo at the Silverado."

"Oh?" He looked at her more closely, his lips pursed.

"Yeah, and I was on a winning streak," she embellished on the spot. "Then the news came and the game ended—"

"Here you are, Andrea," said Helen, bursting breathless beside her. "I've been looking everywhere for you."

The counterman took Helen's passport and asked a few questions that Venus didn't even hear because she was swept away by a giddy feeling that she was going to make it through this.

Helen poked her, breaking her reverie.

"Andi, the man is talking to you."

"Yes?"

"Where were you when the War started?"

"I was . . ." She nearly said *playing bingo at the Silverado*, but caught herself in time. That was a line that could be used for the start of the war or the end of the war, or any point in between, but it couldn't be used twice. What could she say instead?

"Andi," said Helen, prompting her. "You were —"

"It's embarrassing, but we're all adults here," said Venus, to shut her up before she gave it away. Having said that, she tried following the thread she had started. "I was on a date. Viagra and everything."

"Andi!"

Helen was bug-eyed frightened, and the man seemed genuinely surprised.

"Things were going great, but then the news came, and, well, even Viagra couldn't help against a bunch of nukes."

The man closed his mouth with a click. He suddenly became business-like, telling them they had reserved seats on the next maglev from Los Angeles to Seattle, giving them the track number, and handing them their passports and boarding passes.

They walked away, heading for the track. Nobody pursued them, the lines kept moving, everything was normal.

"What just happened, back there?" asked Venus once

the train started. There was nobody sitting next to them.

"You have Alzheimer's, remember dear?" said Helen. "Your memory of old times is very sharp, but you often forget recent events."

"I feel like I've been away for four or five years."

"Yes, that's right," said Helen, smiling and winking. "We came to save Venus but we were too late, and now we are going home."

"I miss Leah."

"So do I, dear," said Helen. "So do I."

•

Everybody blamed it on Dr. Mabuhay, the bio-industrialist who had revolutionized reproduction in 2040. For a nominal price his clinics offered exogenesis as well as standard genefixing. Suddenly the common woman could afford a procedure that for a generation had been available only to the wealthy. Nearly everybody who wanted a baby preferred one who had been cleaned of any genetic defects, a perfect embryo carried to term in an artificial womb until the optimum day of decanting. As a result, Mabuhay clinics sprouted up everywhere. This milestone separated the Mabuhay generation from what would come to be called the Pure generation that had preceded it. When the popularity of children began to decline in 2048, Dr. Mabuhay revved it up again with "genhancement," a patented technique allowing the first designer babies. That period proved to be an Indian Summer, however, and children continued their slide in the polls. Big Birthing collapsed when the Mabuhay scandals broke — the children were said to be defective or "not as advertised," and some were found to be cuckoo kids, literally the offspring of Mabuhay and other franchise owners.

Venus d'Malibu had matured early. In 2053, the year after the scandal, she was twelve but she looked fourteen — five foot two, short and buxom, with dark bedroom eyes, and blondish-brown hair. Geezers who wanted to be her sugar daddy said she looked like Drew Barrymore, whoever that was. On what would turn out to be her last day of school she was in private consultation with the elementary school principal.

"Hey Venus, how about a quickie?"

He sat in his chair, a bachelor in his fifties, looking up at her perched on the edge of his desk. He was cool with Mabuhay kids.

"No, I don't think so," she said, playing with the knot of his necktie.

The door burst open and a cop entered the room to her left. The principal rose up and Venus slid off the desk.

"My, my," said the young cop, swiping at his sandy mustache. "Afternoon delight."

"Can I help you?" said the principal, trying to muster dignity as his face turned red.

"She's a teen?"

"Yes, a teacher's aide," said the principal, lying.

"Maybe you can save me some," said the cop, licking his lips. "We could party. Is lunch hour over?"

"Yes."

"And where are the sixth grade rooms?"

"Upstairs, room 23 and 24. But what's this —"

"Never mind. Keep her warm 'til I get back, *pungyo.*" The cop closed the door as he left.

"Venus, I think you should go home," said the principal, stiffly. "Take the rest of the day off."

"Will we get in trouble?"

"No, but I don't like the look of that guy."

"You don't have to share me, Harv," she said. "Let's just —"

"No, Venus —"

Shots rang out, followed by children's screams and more shots.

Venus ran out of the school, heading for home. She could hear the muffled gunshots continuing for the first block, but the sound fell off after the second block. Still, the familiar streets looked somehow different, suddenly alien and menacing, and police cars were terrifying. She feared the rogue cop was following her on foot, that he would kill both her and Leah at home. She kept looking back but nobody was following her. Everything was normal. By the time she got to her apartment building she was walking and wondering if it had really happened, since it seemed so unreal.

Leah was watching 3V on drugs but she was sober enough to say, "Why you home so early?"

"Something weird happened at school."

"What, did he stick it in your ass?" she asked, cracking a smile.

"No, not like that," said Venus, making a face. Leah was cool, but still. "There was this cop and he started shooting kids, I think."

"Whoa, fuck, hold on." Leah shook her head a few times, trying to clear it. "This just happened?"

"Yeah. Got any mello? I could use a couple."

"Wait a sec, let's check the news first."

"Hey, how come you're home now?" asked Venus as Leah looked for the remote control.

"Another bomb threat at work," she said. "They sent us home. Here it is." She snatched up the remote. "Now, what was I doing?"

"Surfing the news about my school."

"Oh yeah."

Drudge News L.A. had a headline "School Shooting," with the icons for "breaking news" and "developing story" next to it. They followed a link to Drudge News North America and saw similar stories from Boswash, Detroit, and St. Louis. They skimmed the reports and watched eerie clips from security cameras, showing death squads killing kids in elementary schools. At one point Venus noticed a change come over Leah, something more than sudden sobriety in the face of tragedy — she had made a grim decision. But she gave Venus a bunch of mellos to take, and took some herself. They slept well.

At breakfast the next morning, Leah told Venus, "You're not going to school today. We're going to go looking around."

"For what?"

"For something different."

They rode a hydrogen bus out of the San Fernando Valley over to West Hollywood, where they walked into the entrance of a walled compound. Venus thought it was an active seniors enclave, like the one her grandmother Helen was at up in Seattle. But when she saw the guard-house window had blue stars and pink hearts, she knew it was a pedoville.

Inside there was a framed photo of an old president who had been a general during the War, next to a framed copy of his executive decree on pedo rights.

The guard had a big gun and a big smile. He looked like Che Guevara without a mustache.

Leah had to sign a waiver even to stand there and talk. After some boring back and forth with the guard, she told Venus, "I'm going to have a chin-chin in the back. You stay here." She went into a back room to make some arrangements, leaving Venus alone with the guard.

Venus thought about the blue stars and the pink hearts.

"They love girls here, *mei-mei*," the guard said in a way that was respectful to her, almost worshipful. "They have a holiday in summer called Alice Day — have you heard of it?"

"Nah."

"It's a *maskee* holiday, just like Christmas. You should come sometime."

Leah came back out and said, "Vee, you're going to stay here for a while."

"What do you mean?"

"I mean it is very bad out there, and safe in here."

"So we're gonna move here."

"No, *you're* gonna stay here for a while."

"You mean, like, I'm on a *team* here?"

"Yeah."

"I'm not a team player, Mom," said Venus, using the m-word bomb. "I'm a free agent — I work for you."

"You don't work for me." Leah's face was red but she didn't flare up into anger like she normally would.

"What about Harv? He's almost ready to shack up —"

"I'm not interested in Harv," said Leah. "I've never been interested in Harv. That was for you, or for him, but not for me."

"Huh? What are you —?"

"Venus, we need some time apart, okay? I need some *me* time. What you do here won't be any different from the partying we've been doing, it is just safer instead of being free. You see what I mean? You're getting something in exchange for hooking up instead of just doing it for free."

"God, I don't believe this," said Venus, looking away in disgust, trying to keep her feelings of betrayal from flowing out her eyes.

"I know it's sudden, but yesterday, that was some really crazy shit."

"Yeah, it was." Venus took a deep breath, let it out, and looked at Leah, ready to deal. "Okay, so how long."

"A couple weeks? I don't know. I'll watch the news."

That sounded reasonable to Venus. "Wait a second," she said. "I have one question." She turned to the guard. "The stars are for boy-love and the hearts are for girl-love, right?"

"Yes, that's right."

"Okay, so the big star is the man and the little star is the boy."

"Yes."

"So the little heart is the girl and the big heart is a woman? I mean, look, I don't want to get into any lesbo stuff."

"No, not a woman," said the guard. "There are no

women here."

"So it really should be a big blue star and a little pink heart, right?"

"I guess so." He shrugged. "It is just a symbol, an international one."

"And I don't do anal."

"You're not a boy, so it shouldn't be a problem."

"*Toh-shiang*," she said, that popular slang term meaning, "I surrender."

•

Venus settled into the dormitory, finding it a cross between two classics — Hogwarts and a Bangkok brothel. Her partying started the first day, but it was a week before she had to break the rules she had set at the beginning.

Venus left the morning after, taking the bus back to her apartment. On the ride she mentally rehearsed the argument she was going to have with Leah, about how there was no way in hell she was going back there again.

Her keycard wouldn't open the apartment door. She pounded on the door to vent frustration, on the off-chance that Leah was home — after all, the curtains were open. Nobody opened the door. She looked in the window and saw that the front room was empty.

She went to the manager, who told her that Leah had moved out a week ago.

"I got a few bags of your stuff, if you want 'em."

"I want Leah," said Venus, a few tears skipping down her cheeks. "Where'd she go?"

"I don't know," he said, shrugging. "She wouldn't say."

She used his phone to call Leah at work. The woman who answered said Leah wasn't there and she gave Venus the runaround.

Venus rode the bus to Leah's workplace, hoping to catch her there, but security would not let her in, nor would they give any information about employees, current or previous. They wouldn't even call Leah — if she were there or not.

Venus wondered if Leah was shacking up with Harv after all, so she burned up the last of her money on a bus ride over to his bungalow. Harv was there since school was already out for the day, but he said he hadn't seen Leah, and he let Venus search the place.

When she told him about the pedoville, he said, "That sounds like the best." So he wasn't going to even offer to take her in or anything. She was disgusted and figured that Leah was right to pass him by — she was probably hooking up with movie people like she wanted, probably living out in Malibu like she always dreamed. Venus bummed some bus fare off of him and left.

Night was falling as she rode the bus. Her choice had narrowed down to either the pedoville or the street. What would she do on the street? She'd be homeless so she'd have to get an iPhone, despite the certainty of getting brain cancer from it. She'd be a *jianhuo*, a streetwalker, or in some gang. That didn't sound good, and death squads killed street kids all the time.

She went back to the pedoville.

•

"I hate Leah for leaving . . . Venus at that place," said Venus.

Helen was silent for a few moments. "But don't you see she was right?" she asked. "Those places have been safe, up until now. Not all Libertarians are pedos, but all pedos are Libertarians. We almost made it in time to save poor Venus."

"I thought she was just getting too old to stay," said Venus.

"Well, there's that, too," admitted Helen. "But mainly it was Leah dying last month — of drugs, mind you — and the way things are heating up. I think they are shutting that place down before the white coats do it for them."

"Those girls weren't really girl scouts."

"Of course not," said Helen. "They were snatched from a pedoville and forced to wear those uniforms."

"But why? How did it get like this?"

"I don't know," said Helen. "The pendulum swings from one extreme to the opposite. This Purity Revolution has probably reached its limit now and the pendulum will head back. If Venus could — could *have* made it to nineteen or twenty, she would have been safe." She glanced around for white coats, then leaned close and spoke softly. "Twenty-year olds killing children — it's a lethal sibling rivalry, is what it is. They were told they were special, but the evil doctor devalued that identity, which was all they had. It's a class warfare of spoiled rich, hand-made *brats* against cheap, mass-produced upstarts."

"It seems so . . . strange," said Venus, watching the Central Valley flash by outside the window. "Like a fairy tale, a dark fairy tale — like Hansel and Gretel."

"That's just how it is, and the ovens are always full. Don't forget it."

An anti-youth mood gripped North America, from Alaska to Durango. During Venus's stay in the pedoville sanctuary, the simmering cauldron outside had boiled over into a different stage, going beyond circumspect liquidations into full-blown revolutionary horror. Mabuhay kids were even blamed for the avian flu epidemic — the so-called "Chinese Revenge." It was an unusual era of Medea and Saturn, where slaughter of the "unclean" and "defective" children was accepted as a necessary evil; a time when white coats proudly posed with rifles beside trophy stacks of dead ferals in the remains of their woodland hideouts.

Venus saw the lack of a public gallows at the Seattle train station, and she took it as a good sign. Seattle was a world of water bordered by land — from the hilltop of Helen's place she could see the Puget Sound to the west, with land right behind it, and Lake Washington to the east, with land right behind it. Blue water, green pine trees. It was so different from what she had known before, the separated areas of land and water in Southern California — the semi-arid Valley and the wild, unbounded ocean at Malibu. It was a tidy blend that was immediately comforting to her.

Venus stayed with Helen in her tiny apartment for a few days, learning the ropes. Out on the street she met and mingled with other girls in disguise, and even some boys. She discovered that her education at the pedoville had given her many skills that the street kids did not have, and knowledge is power, which led her to grudgingly accept her time there as a gift, as Helen had suggested. Finding the city more tolerant of her kind so long as she stayed in disguise, Venus moved out and made a living for herself, visiting Helen once a month or so.

Two years later the generation cleansing fever began to ebb across the continent. A promising new reproductive technology was being tested. Attacks by both ferals and white coats were down. There was talk of amnesty for ferals and unclean. The moderate Pures, now in their triumphant thirties, expressed a certain optimism. They spoke of a fresh start despite the new energy rationing — a new generation of "golden ones" created and nurtured by the new technique. "Nurture" was a buzzword, the latest view on the Mabuhay mess being that the kids were regarded as objects by mothers who hadn't gone through the chemical transformation and bonding of labor, delivery, and lactation. The new system that addressed these problems passed all testing and the first new babies were decanted in 2060.

Venus d'Malibu was nineteen disguised as ninety when a car pulled up beside her on the street one spring day at noon.

"I got a quick job, pays cash," said the guy in the car. "You interested?"

With her hands on her padded hips, she leaned forward

to get a look at him. The guy looked safe, a clean-shaven man in his 40s with gray streaks in his hair. She shrugged.

"Sure," she said. "Coding and spamming is $100 an hour, genehacking is $200."

"I was thinking of something else."

"Babysitting is $100."

"I was hoping for a hook up."

"Are you a cop?"

"No, just a lonely salesman passing through town."

"Yeah, all right. What kind of action are you looking for?"

"Fifty-fifty."

"That'll be a hundred. Up front."

"Okay."

"Show me the money," she said. "Yeah, all right. You got to bring me back here after." She got into the car, putting her cane between them and her granny purse on her lap. "Where you want to do it? Rainer Beach High is good, not so ratty as the middle schools."

"There's a quiet place, over by Victory Park. I'd like to do it outside."

The car pulled away from the curb.

"Okay."

"Can you really do that stuff?" the John asked. "Coding, spamming, and genehacking?"

"Not that well," she admitted, "but there's a lot of basic grunt work, bottle washing and shit, I can do that."

"You're a gray girl, right?"

"Yeah. That's why you hired me, isn't it?"

"Sure," he said. "I just get so tired of old pussy. Even though the new method is here, I'll still have to wait twelve years for the golden ones to come online."

"Yeah, it's a real hard row to hoe," she said, looking at him. He laughed at that. "And that's where I make my money."

"Do you have a pimp?"

"No," she said, looking out the window. "I'm on my

own."

"I bet you have a pimp," said the John. "He's a big tough feral who slaps you around."

"Whatever turns you on," she said, rolling her eyes.

"You really don't have a pimp?"

"Nope."

They got on I-5, heading south.

"What are you going to do with amnesty next week?" he asked.

"Same as I'm doing now, only without all this junk."

"Still be a hooker?" he said. "Yeah, I can see that. The money will get better, I'm sure."

"The dirty work is where the money is," she said. "Maybe I'll be a nanny or something."

"A nanny?" he laughed. "Really? Wouldn't you be, you know, tempted to kill 'em?"

"No, of course not."

"Huh." He pondered for a moment, then asked, "Do you have experience in that?"

"No," she said. "But it can't be that hard."

They rode in silence for about twenty miles before getting off at S 272nd Street and the ruins of Star Lake. Camelot Park, a few miles further south, had been nuked at the start of the War by an errant warhead. While the War was still being fought, the resulting four square miles of destruction around Camelot had been declared a Victory Park, as so many of them had been in those days.

The John drove them to a woodsy little spot, an access road just off S 272nd Street, which bordered the northern edge of the park. He got out, stretched, and sniffed the air.

"Yeah, this is good," he said. "Get out. Let's do it here."

She got out of the car, glanced around at forty years worth of scrub growth and towering pines. It was hard to believe a hundred thousand civilians had died there in an instant, but then she saw the crumbling corner of a ruinous house not more than forty feet away.

"Give me the money," she said.

He handed it over. She put it in her granny purse.

They heard a car approach on the road above, hidden from sight by a steep embankment. He froze, listening for it to slow for the service road turn-off, but it went on and away.

"Let's get started," she said.

"Take off all your clothes first," he said.

"You're the boss." She leaned her cane against the car, and took off her solar hood. "You got a blanket or something? I don't want to get poked in the back." She started taking off her geriatric dress, the usual long sleeve garment made of high SPF cloth, and the edge of her frump suit was exposed.

"All I have is this," said the John, holding up a hand towel. "For cleaning up after. We'll do it doggy style."

With the dress cast aside, she struggled out of her frump suit and removed all doubts about her real age, revealing a ripe teenage body with big breasts, flat tummy, and bubble butt. Her face and hands were still old.

"Here, take off your makeup," he said, tossing her the towel.

"No," she snapped, tossing it back. "It takes forever to put it back on."

"Okay, well, take off your shoes."

"It'll cost you extra."

"Sure."

When she took off her second sock he said, "Thick ankles. Mark of Mabuhay."

She dropped the sock and sashayed over to him.

"I'll *Mabuhay* you," she purred, then she knelt before him, using the cane to steady herself.

"You don't need that here," said the John. "The cane."

"Yes, I do," she said. "I got bad knees — I really need it to get back up."

She got to work. She had hoped that the free strip show she had provided would make her job easier, but it didn't, so she had to spend more time than usual in prepping him.

When he was ready he pushed her away, then moved into position behind her. She dropped forward so her hands rested on the cane lying on the weedy ground.

"Hey, can I use that towel for my knees?" she asked.

He didn't answer, so she let it slide.

When he started doing his thing back there, Venus automatically entered the zone, the unfeeling place where she waited things out. She thought about old times, before the pedoville, when she thought that Harv might live with her and her mom. She thought about her mom, and how when she found out Venus was fooling around with boys, she took her out partying and hooked her up with men.

The John suddenly stopped and said, "Car."

Her reverie interrupted, she looked over her right shoulder to watch the top of the embankment. She felt the twisted towel loop over her head, onto her neck. Her alarm became panic when the loop tightened.

Venus felt blood bulging in her head like a balloon about to pop when she moved to lift the cane up for a jab at him. He countered by lying on her back, bearing her down with his weight so her arms couldn't lift anything. Her ears were ringing as she crumpled to the right, dropping them both to the ground with a thud, but he held on tight. She felt a numbing weakness growing in her hands. She twisted the cane handle and drew out the dagger hidden within. She slashed back at his hands holding the towel, heard him gasp with surprise and pain as she cut him.

His grip weakened for an instant.

She broke free, jumped up, and ran for the upper road, gasping for breath. She had a head start as he pulled up his pants, but then he gave chase. When she started scrambling up the embankment she heard him closing in, fast. She cried out when he grabbed her ankle and yanked. She slid down and kicked him full in the face with her free foot, escaping again.

She clawed her way up and got onto the road, running east, with him coming close behind. A familiar car was coming toward them in the other lane, a car full of bearded men, and the John growled with an extra burst of speed. Venus sensed his fingers reaching for her hair.

The car screeched to a halt at close range and three guys piled out, waving pistols around, while the driver stayed behind the wheel.

"Hey, she's — god damn it!" The John was giving up on the chase and cursing his luck.

Venus jumped into the back seat.

"Wow, you okay, boss?" asked Octavian, the driver.

"I think we got a live one," she said, gingerly touching her burning neck. "Fucker tried to choke me."

The John was clearly surprised by what she had done. She saw how it dawned on him that two of the guys were small, like jockeys, and then he saw their beards were grease paint. Then he knew.

"Hey, I —"

"Shut up," said Angel, the tallest one, brandishing his 9mm automatic pistol. "Get on the hood."

"But I —"

The feral eighteen-year-old cocked the hammer back.

"Sit on the fucking hood, John. We're going for a ride. To your car."

The John sat on the hood.

"The car's right down there?" asked Octavian as the boys got back in the car.

"Yeah," said Venus.

"You okay, Andi?" asked Angel out the side of his mouth, keeping his eyes on the John as the car started forward.

"Fucker tried to choke me with a towel," said Venus. Octavian did a sharp U-turn that nearly tumbled the John off, and they headed east.

"Sorry we lost you," said Angel.

"I'm glad you came back — it was just in time."

The car turned right onto the service road and followed it west. The John's car came into view, parked face-out for a quick getaway, and Octavian parked their car head to head with it, blocking it in.

Venus hopped out on the left and dashed over to her clothing. She heard Angel get out and say, "Over on this side, John. Let's give Andi some privacy."

Skipping the frump suit, Venus threw on the dress, then stepped into the panties.

"Now John, we don't mind fellows fucking our women, so long as they pay," said Angel. "But Andi tells me you tried to choke her."

"I'm sorry, I got carried away," the John said. "I wasn't really going to hurt her."

Venus, carrying the frump suit on the other side, made a face at him. She tossed the suit into the backseat, picked up her gun purse, and started walking back to her stuff.

"*Toh-shiang, toh-shiang*," said Angel. "It's just going to cost you extra."

"Sure."

"Nice car."

"Uh, thanks."

Back at the spot, Venus stood for a moment looking at the scatter of stuff — the treacherous hand towel, her shoes and socks, her granny purse, the stick part of her cane. A bad thing had happened, but it could have been worse. She smiled at the thought of getting a car out of it, as Angel was hinting.

"What you got in the trunk?" said Angel.

"Here, I'll open it —" said the John.

"No, Rat opens it. Give him the keys."

Rat, the smallest of the ferals, handed his .22 caliber revolver to Duncan and approached the John with his hand out. Close up, the twelve-year-old was obviously a genhancement defective. The John gave him the keys, shrinking back from physical contact.

"Okay, let's all move to the back, past the trunk," said Angel.

Venus was now sitting on the ground, putting on her socks. She saw the John glance over his left shoulder to see Octavian drifting along with them over on the other side of the car with his gun drawn.

Rat came around and put the key into the trunk lock.

"Keep moving, John," said Angel.

Rat opened the trunk and announced, "A lot of junk. Three coolers, some tools, a pile of rags."

"Okay, John," said Angel when the man was fifteen feet past the trunk. Angel kept five feet away from him. "Stop there and turn around."

Venus was putting on her shoes. The John was twelve feet away from her. Venus saw the John taking it all in. He was scared, but not scared enough. She could almost see his mind working, counting the guns on him, doing the math, and when his eyes flicked over at her she flashed her panties at him to throw him off. He didn't seem to notice. That was a bad sign.

"What kind of tools?" asked Angel.

"Saw, a chainsaw, a bolt cutter," said Rat, leaning into the open cavity. "Shit like that."

"Outdoorsy stuff," said Angel. "This is a nice place for a picnic. Check the coolers, Rat."

Venus saw the John stir at that, and her senses came alert. As Rat wrestled the top off a cooler she kept her left hand fooling with the laces of her shoe but let her right hand drop onto the target pistol lying on her skirt, hidden from the John.

"Nothing but ice," said Rat.

"Check the next one," said Angel, his eyes narrowed. Venus was glad to see him take a sharper interest in the John — he saw it, too. The John was playing it cool but he was still telegraphing something.

Rat pulled off the top of the second cooler and yelled, "Holy shit!"

Duncan and Octavian looked down into the trunk, and Angel, distracted by the alarm in the boy's voice, started to turn. In that instant the John sprang forward, grabbing Angel's gun and knocking him down. Venus brought her pistol up. The John was so focused on taking out Duncan's two guns he didn't notice Venus until she shot him in the chest.

The John whirled toward her, blindsided, and he suddenly looked like Harv but she shot him again anyway. He raised the pistol toward her as he started to fall backward, and he looked like her dad but she shot him a third time, part of a fusillade as the boys belatedly opened up.

"Okay, okay!" shouted Angel from the ground. "Guns up!"

He jumped up and yelled, "Goddamn it, Rat! You nearly got us killed!" He went over to the John and took his gun back, red-faced and muttering obscenities.

Venus tried to stand but felt woozy so she dropped back down. She felt numb and weepy.

"But there's a *head* in the cooler," said Rat. "A girl's *head.*"

"Sick fuck." Angel dug through the John's pockets, tossing the passport to Venus because she could read. She flipped it open and felt a full-body icy wash.

"Bounty hunter," she said.

"Still a sick fuck."

"Another girl's head in the last one," said Rat.

"He's only in his fucking thirties," said Venus, her voice sounding far away to her. "He's a Pure but he's dressed like he's older."

The boys closed in on the man, forming a ragged circle. Angel touched the John's gray streaks. "Hey, check it out. It's like paint, not even dye."

"He's in camo," said Rat. "Like a hunter."

The John started moaning. Spooked, they all unloaded on him. Thunder and fire.

"Fuck, we got to get out of here," said Angel, waving

his hand for a breath of air in the sudden cloud of gun smoke. "We take his car, we leave the heads."

"We take the heads," said Venus.

"Are you crazy?"

"They're our sisters," said Venus, starting to weep.

"So what?"

"So we bury them."

"*Toh-shiang, toh-shiang,*" he said, walking over to her, flushed and excited. "You and me will take the new car, Octavian and the rest in the other. Come on — hey!" He dropped into a crouch before her, suddenly concerned. "Are you all right?"

"I feel sick," she said. "Real sick."

His face screwed up in thought for a moment. He glanced back at the others, then pitched his voice softly so only she could hear, and said, "I'm sorry I let you down, back there."

"No, no, you did good," she said. "I just never shot a guy before, that's all."

"And that was some good shooting, too. Fuck!"

"Thanks —"

"I mean, bam-bam-bam!"

"But, aw . . ."

"Hey, listen," he said. "You didn't kill him, okay? He deserved it, but we did it, me and the boys."

"Yeah, okay." Normally she would bridle at others taking credit for something she had done, but in this case it really felt better.

"So come on, old lady. Time to go home."

"Help me up," she said with a little smile. "And tell me — do you think my ankles are thick?"

I, MOMBOT

I was a sleepwalker as a boy. During the year we lived at a house with a swimming pool my mother feared that I would sleepwalk into the deep end one night and drown.

At the moment I'm drowning in the pool of parenting. It is Monday night and my workaholic wife Lyn is late getting home; the special dinner of spaghetti carbonara has gone cold and sticky, while the Baked Alaska is a warming mess. The shrieking you hear is not me, it is Grenich, my one-year-old daughter. She wants to be fed and I guess there's no point in making her wait for Lyn.

I need to find daycare for Grenich. I've been watching at the tot park, talking to the nannybots who I see there every day, but there are no openings. It's time to tell Lyn to search among her officemates. In the meantime let's do some breathing exercises and visualize a serenity garden.

Hello, young men, I'm Jason Dee. Welcome to my brave new world.

It wasn't like this at first. When Grenich was born the world was suddenly newly minted, vibrantly shimmering, and full of wonder. Over time we learned that she was colicky, but for three months there were two of us to care for her. The maternity leave ended, mommy went back to work with breast pump in hand, and I was alone.

"I can do this," I said. "I can do this." The little engine that could.

Infant care is inherently difficult for everyone, even housewives with milk-laden breasts. Colicky babies are extra difficult. What is colic, Spock?

Big mystery; no simple answer; case by case.

In layman's terms?

The baby is fussy and cannot be consoled. The condition usually disappears by age three months, but it can persist to age six months or more. It is not rare for the colicky baby to sleep all night but cry off and on for half the day.

That sounds like my case.

Be glad she doesn't cry half the night.

Good point.

The first day! The first week! "I can do this." *Yes, but how long can you tread water?*

In the very beginning it was hard. I was new at it, so I'm sure I was exuding that old "fresh meat" pheromone. The first few weeks of going for a morning stroll brought us a number of things: from the common "So *Monsieur Mère* is taking care of you today?" of shop keepers and market clerks, to more cutting episodes . . .

— We were on the main street of town, near the monorail. Little Grenich was crying and I was trying both to calm her down and discover the source of her distress. A wisecracking white-haired old guy passing by on the sidewalk said, as if speaking for baby, "'You're not mommy.'"

— We were strolling along the edge of Monorail Park. There was a gray-haired guy jogging with a little girl in a jogging stroller. Daughter, granddaughter; first-family, third-family, who knows? We exchanged pleasantries as they jogged past us and when they stopped at the crossing light we caught up.

At this point a woman in a calico dress was crossing the street from the left. She called out, "Wow, guys are taking care of babies! Far out! Viva la revolution!" She had a big black dog on a rope. The dog's muzzle was bound shut with dark tape. The jogger ignored her. She kept on talking loudly. "This is great. Back when I was having babies, all the guys were off at the war."

— A few blocks up from Monorail Way was a new child-friendly café called "Crayon." I wheeled her in there so I could have a simple early lunch away from home. The place was empty except for the cashier. Grenich was watching the aquarium, I was eating a sandwich roll, when in came "helmet guy," a tall street freak who wears a motorcycle helmet as he stalks around town. He came right over to my table, sat down across from me, and told me that I need to get some marketable skills before it is too late, that I should join the army, they will give me some skills. The woman, God bless her, chased him out, and came back to say, "I'm sorry. Are you okay? What did he say?" "Nothing," I said. "He's just talking. I'm fine." But inside I knew he was right.

. . . the town itself became an antagonist, reacting to my new role with antibodies. Even though I had been living there for six years it had changed into a strange place where I was new in town.

At the end of the first month I was negotiating with Lyn.

"No, I can't do this on the weekends, too," I said. "You have to do it. And do the laundry, and the shopping, and the cooking, and the cleaning."

She agreed to everything and did what she could. It lasted two weekends, because living in an apartment makes laundry impossible on weekends, so I went back to washing on Thursdays, and the one who does the cooking should do the shopping, so I went back to shopping. I still had my weekends free and I tried to get back to my landscape paintings: with my window overlooking gasoline alley I worked at forests and streams.

I kept thinking that things would be easier if we only had a house. What I really needed was some family support but there was none. We were "on our own" as much as if we were in a foreign country.

•

So here we are, it is Friday and we're all eating dinner on time. Nothing fancy, just a tuna casserole the way my mom used to make. I'm so excited because daycare is just around the corner, I keep waiting for the news, trying to ask, and finally I do: "So, any word on daycare?"

Her shoulders slump. "Sorry, I forgot to ask."

"How could you forget all *week?* Now we've got a weekend of nothing when we could have been making some progress!"

"I'll do it on Monday."

"I can't believe this," I say, the anger surging through me.

Take a deep breath. Visualize the breath as a golden light . . .

How did I get here? We met in college a few miles from here. She wrote songs and played the guitar back then. One of her songs talked about how heavenly a "50-50 household" would be if only men would do the dishes and help with the children, and it sounded so reasonable in college. Was that it, a siren's song that led me to this whirlpool?

Or were the seeds planted earlier?

I wanted to be an astronaut.

In my serenity garden I come across a tracing I had done as a preschooler, a smiling astronaut in a silver white space suit that had those mysterious hoses on the outside. He is smooth at the groin, the blank crotch of Apollo instead of the disturbingly long zipper, the toothed vagina of Gemini.

The space program rose to a few lunar landings and fell, leaving me with nothing but a trunk full of stories for boys, the stories themselves trying to come to terms with the lost dream, like off-key bards singing of fallen Camelot.

No manned missions to Mars, not even a Moon base, nothing. The vision darkened, the hazards of space became so hard that self-sacrifice was required of the astronauts: cyborg spacemen, men cut off from their feelings, who had to check dials and gauges to see what they felt; neutered spacers, men who had given up their reproductive organs for space travel; androids, wholly synthetic men who could weather the interstellar transit to land on a planet and bring some human embryos to term in an artificial womb, thus achieving interstellar colonization by way of robots and seeds.

I had never wanted to be a robot, I wanted to be a spaceman, but in the cultural dream spacemen had become robots, and robots were slaves.

And so by a circuitous path I awoke one day to find myself a fully biological, non-female "Mombot," a new model in a world (or a town, at least) that did not know what to do with me. I was like one of those androgynous spacers, stepping out of the silver sphere that had brought me down to Earth, and the people wondered: What will we call it? Should we address it at all?

I often wished that I could turn off my ears so I couldn't hear the colicky baby wail the day away (in her vibrating chair in the dry bathtub with the white noise of the ceiling fan); turn off my nose when dealing with diapers; turn a dial to slow my heart; slide a lever to cool my brain.

I wanted a house. More than that, I wanted my mother.

Inside a dream I was inside a house. A small house, but it belonged to Lyn and me. I was alone in the entry hallway, blond hardwood floor beneath my feet and sunlight streaming in through both the half-open front door and the many-paned window of the sitting room to the right. Lyn was nearby but not present.

The ghost of my mother arose from Grenich sleeping on the floor. She was standing before me and I was happy to see her, but she became agitated.

"Why am I here?" she asked. "I was free but now I'm

trapped. Why?"

"I don't know," I lied.

She began to leave the floor.

"How long?" she said.

"It has been ten years," I said.

"Ten years!" she shrieked, arcing toward the ceiling and coming down like a wave toward me. "And you called me back — no!" She roared past me and into the living room where she knocked vases off the mantle. They shattered on the floor as she turned to make another charge at me.

I left my body and flew into the sitting room, where I fled through the window. She chased after me, and another me chased after her chasing me.

The front lawn was actually a backyard, and I hovered a few inches over the bright green grass, enjoying the beauty of it and the exhilaration of floating — it had been so long I thought I'd never fly again. But it seemed that I should go further, so I flew over the fence and kept going up. Dodging the deadly power lines, swimming up into the free air. Higher, higher — how high could I go?

I guess I flew west over the bay, since I looked down onto San Francisco. There was the red bridge, there was the black bridge, and there were the tiny cars like ants. Some white beach cliffs captured my attention, so I swooped down to land. Closer, closer, and then I was driving a large brown luxury sedan from the beach.

The engine was having trouble. I came to an intersection and the engine died. I got out and pushed it with hands that had become as brown as the car. I was no longer white. I became aware of the watchful eyes of the police in their squad car, seeing an African-American guy pushing a luxury car through an intersection. At first it was a strain, but it grew less and less as the car shrank smaller and smaller, shading greener and greener. As I maneuvered it out of the busy crossroad I was able to jump in for a running start. It worked. I pedaled happily away.

The police pulled me over two blocks later.

45

Now it was like a black movie screen. On the upper left a cameo circle opened up with the white policeman's face in three-quarters profile.

"Well, we got somebody," he said.

Below the first, another cameo circle opened up with my black guy's face in three-quarters profile. "I didn't do nothing," he said.

"Is this the one?" said the cop.

In the upper right a new circle opened, this one with a weepy brunette. "Yes," she said. "That's the man who raped me!"

"What do you have to say for yourself?" asked the cop, looking down.

"Oh, she's pretty an' all," said the accused, "but I'd much rather do it with you." Batting his eyelashes.

Fade to black.

Fade in to extreme close-up of brunette's face in profile, the visible left eye opened wide and tracking slowly. Pull back to see more of her face, revealing her dark hair in disarray over the white tiles. Her lips are moving slightly but there is no sound. Pull back enough to see that she is the subject of a vivisection. Blood everywhere below the shoulder line. At the upper right periphery of vision appear the blue trousers around ankles, the bared pink buttocks of a body stuffed into a medical waste can. Camera pan left to the African-American guy wiping his hands on a bloodied towel.

How will he get out of this predicament? He is in the heart of an installation, a police station, a hospital, or a police hospital.

Calmly he picks up the wall phone, touches the digits for an outside number. Waits, and then speaks.

"Hello, it's me. They picked me up on a petty traffic violation and, well . . . things got out of hand. Certain things were said, certain things were done. The party is over but now there is a mess. Send over the clean squad."

Cut to a still shot of three of the seven deadly Finns,

dressed up in frilly tutus and leather corsets . . . I woke up laughing at the idea that these guys will be able to inconspicuously infiltrate the installation, erase sign and symbol of multiple murder, and help the killer escape.

Infant care is inherently difficult for everyone, even pre-soccer moms with grandparents on call. Grenich grew out of strolling as the season progressed, so we spent more time at the tot lot, a small neighborhood playground. I found a broom and swept the sand from the sidewalks everyday. I learned to bring plastic baggies to pick up the cat poop and cigarette butts. I came to know the regulars, a half-dozen daycare nannybots with their young charges and three couples (a translator, a teacher, a chef) with their children. Even in this sand garden, flawed manifestation of my serenity garden, there were still disturbing signals . . .

— the teacher's wife caught us by the tot park one morning, walked me through the usual Q&A routine without mentioning *Monsieur Mère* (thank God), and then gushed:

"That's really great. Things are so much easier now! My husband tried to do it with his first daughter seven, or no, eight years ago now, and it was too hard. Now he sees her once or twice a month."

— Another white-haired old guy told me, "You are doing the right thing. It's terrible that children today are being raised by robots." Which I thought was nice at first but bigoted on second thought. Then again, later on Pat said exactly the same thing, and coming from a nannybot it had particular weight at the same time it was a hypocritical paradox.

— That time at the tot park when there were two pre-soccer moms we hadn't seen before, sitting together and talking like they do at the cafes on the main street. And the boy, maybe almost two years old, saw me and walked over, drawn into my orbit, showing me his cement mixer truck toy, while my daughter had crawled away as she always did.

"Yes, truck," I said. "That is a truck. Oh, I can hold it?

Hmm, yes, this is a truck all right. Here you go, have your truck."

One of the moms looks up and calls out, "He's always like this around guys." Then she goes back into the huddle. The words, the attitudes (the self-absorbed indifference of the moms; the driving need of the toddler), the scenario made me sad. Were there no regularly scheduled guys in this child's life? What was the fate of this boy, and how did it mirror my own fate as a boy and now as a guy?

. . . I carved my niche, yet the town was still adjusting.

By the end of the season I was negotiating with Lyn again. Even though she was in charge of baby care on weekends, the fact that I was in the apartment meant that I was there to assist. Where was that "50-50" heaven? She should have to put in the same sort of hard time that I did.

"I have to get out of here," I said, avoiding eye contact. "It feels like a prison. So here's my idea — one weekend a month I go car camping. I'm gone the whole time, I do my decompressing out in the wilds, and I come back recharged for another month."

She didn't like it but she agreed to it after I used my last zinger: "If I can't paint landscapes anymore I'd like to at least rest in one, once a month."

The first time I drove away I went to the Sierra foothills and felt the weight lift off of me a little each mile. When I got to the campground I took out a new sketchpad and drew in the fading light. Tears came to my eyes and I wept in relief and self-pity.

•

Now Lyn has been following daycare leads at her office for a few weeks, but nothing has panned out yet. It is depressing. I thought I was at the end of a long slog, but it just keeps going on with no relief in sight. Each oasis is just a mirage. Two steps forward, one step back: every new solution proves to be only barely adequate.

For example, my weekends away: Sometimes the campground is dominated by a loud party, other times I awake at night to find raccoons or a skunk going through my stuff. And Lyn dodges the bullet by making her solo duties into "quality time" exercises of overindulgence and excess. I'd like to strangle the person who came up with the phrase "quality time" — I try to explain to Lyn that there is no such thing, that there is only *time*, and it is generally *hard* time. Am I wrong to want her to suffer a fraction of what I do? Am I twisted to insist on a 50-50 hell? Why must I be insulted by her making it look so easy, as if such frantic activity could be sustained over five consecutive days, week after week, month after month? Why does she act like a grandparent?

The long slog of the last nine months. The colic left a few months ago, one of many things to be thankful for. The town has adjusted to me, or I've become hardened against those words, or more likely, I've found my place within the organism. I've become a minor celebrity, "the guy who sweeps the park." A half-step up from the street freaks, maybe on par with "the guy who waves at cars" or a "cat lady."

Childcare is inherently difficult — just look at what happened to the three couples of the park over this period: the translator's family bought a house, a big change from their one-bedroom apartment on gasoline alley, but then they suddenly divorced (she kept the house); the chef's family placed their girl with one of the lot's nannybots, but then the chef had a nervous breakdown, so the wife took the child and moved out of state (back to her mother's house); the teacher's wife became a soccer mom to his second family in their house up on Monorail Way.

Every three months or so, Lyn had to do some business travel for four days. Which meant that I had to take care of the baby entirely by myself. The nights were especially hard.

One such night I was too tired to think or sleep so I

turned on the TV. I watched some comedy shows that featured appalling stereotypes. But the part that really got me was the caregivers: all female or robot. Guys simply could not change a diaper or bottle-feed an infant — and after several "hilarious consequences" ending in failure, the *Monsieur Mère* guy would cheat and fake an attitude of accomplishment, like it was such a big damn deal that he'd *lie* in order to wear that "medal."

Guys couldn't shop for food, or cook, or do laundry, or make a bed, either. As if boys didn't learn how to cook when the adults of the house stopped cooking, or do the laundry when the adults stopped laundering, or buy food when the adults didn't come home. Or that the boys forgot all these skills as they grew up into guys.

Anyway, I escaped each of those channels and eventually found myself watching a nature show. It was an episode about primates. They were on location in India or somewhere in Asia where apes are sacred, and there was this group of boys throwing rocks into a tree. They hit the female baboon and she fell out of the tree and died. The boys ran away.

The baboon was dead, but its little baby was still alive and crying. Enter "Flint," a mature male baboon. At first the filmmakers thought Flint was going to eat the orphan because he ambled right over and picked it up. But instead, Flint held it close, apparently trying to comfort it, and kept prodding the dead one while looking around for any other possible mother.

The little one quieted down and tried to suckle at Flint's flat nipple. Flint tried to feed his adopted ward small bits of the things that he ate, but the little one was still on a milk only diet.

"Flint," I thought. "You're going to have to think a way around this one. The direct approach is not going to work. Flint, listen to me — find a nursing mother and make her take the orphan. Beat her mate if you have to, but do it now. Find milk, Flint, find milk!"

After a few days, with the little one getting weaker and weaker, the orphan finally died. And Flint, clearly distraught, continued carrying the dead infant around.

My face was wet so I turned off the TV and went to bed.

At the bottom of the maelstrom, amid the wreckage of houseboats and the skeletons of marriages, I realized that my life was really over. I would never be an artist; I would never be an astronaut. The future of bright potential had evaporated. I was alone and there was no help.

•

Which brings us up to date, young men. There is a certain relief in failure, in calling out for help finally. But then it gets irritating in the lack of response and finally it boils down to bargaining.

The calendar says September and Lyn says, "How about an unlicensed nannybot?"

"A back-alley nannybot? My God."

"There are no other openings!"

"All right, we'll take it." One day a week.

Now the calendar says November, and Grenich is at daycare two days a week. We are at this place downtown, trying to get the finances to buy a house. Our economic lives, our net social worth, are detailed on the pages in front of him, the guardian of the gate. He looks them over and then he looks at me, the invisible man whom even the pediatrician avoids looking at, and he says to me, as if Lyn is not sitting next to me, "You should get a job."

Meaning: this situation is not natural; this is not working.

We take it without a fuss, but when we walk out we are crushed.

Now the calendar says January first and Lyn has new conviction.

"We will get a house this year," she says. "And can we

try to have another baby?"

Bargaining, bargaining. It took years to get pregnant last time, it will probably take years again.

•

"So you have two now?" She is sitting in a chair in the living room.

"Mom," I say, rising onto my elbows on the couch. "How did you —?"

"I let myself in," she says. "You were expecting me."

"Yeah," I say. "Yeah, there are the two kids, the house. They're napping, but let me get them up —"

"No, no," she says. "Let them sleep. Shhh."

"It's good to see you."

"It is wonderful to see you," she says. Her smile falters. "I'm sorry about the last time, I don't know what got into me."

"That's okay," I say. "It was hard for me, too."

"But isn't it harder now, with two?"

"Yes, yes it is," I admit.

"Twice as hard?"

"No, it must be five times as hard," I say. "It is so much harder now that it makes everything before look easy."

"Even though you have the house now."

"The house helps," I say. "More room, the laundry, the back yard. And it is quieter." A monorail train roars by, strobbing the afternoon light and rattling the windows.

She laughs.

"That?" I say. "It is white noise, like the sound of surf."

"Amazing," she says, shaking her head. "A person can get used to anything."

I sigh.

"I said I didn't know what got into me before, but I think I do," she says. "No, I do know." She takes a breath. "I never wanted this for you at all. I was a Technofem, I felt that every home should have a nannybot, not just the elites."

"Well. . . ." I say with a shrug.

"So that was my first problem," she says. "I found you in a role I never wanted for you. Something I did not wish on anybody! Something I could not do myself."

"Mom . . ."

"That was my second problem. The fact that you could do — could do what I could not do, and could do it without any of the help I had — well! It cut me deeply, more deeply than I like to admit. It made me feel like I was a Bad Mother."

"No, no, you weren't a Bad Mother," I say.

"Oh?" she smiles as she wiped a tear away. "Who is lying now?"

"I was bitter as a teenager," I say. "That is a common experience. But in my twenties I forgave everything."

"Before I —?"

"Before and after."

"So," she says. "Nothing changed in your forgiveness as you started raising your own child?"

I shudder as I realize she is right. "It's true, the forgiveness . . . went away." It is stunning. I struggle to put it into words. "As I went through . . . each stage . . . I saw the choices you had made. I saw it from a new perspective, as a parent, and my resentment reappeared. Oh Mom, how could you?"

We are both crying.

"Yes, that's right," she says. "That's awareness — that sugar-coating you were trying to feed me before was a product of your own denial." She takes a breath and shakes herself. "The answer is that I did the best I could. Your step-grandmother took care of you through kindergarten. In a way, you are a war between me and her, a war I guess she won."

"Then we moved and I was a latch-key kid in first grade!"

"You had a baby-sitter in the afternoon," she snaps. "But yes, you locked the door behind you, you walked to school by yourself, you walked home by yourself after school, you let yourself in . . . the world was a different place. Such things may be unthinkable today, but it wasn't all that easy then, either." She looks at the blank wall. "Does it help if I tell you that when your sister was born I wept for you? It was clear at that moment that I would be a housewife, imprisoned, buried alive from then on, and I regretted that I was going to do that for two when I could have done that for one. For you."

"You did the best you could."

"Yes, I did," she says. "I tried so hard for so long, which was only four years, and then I couldn't take it anymore. Another marriage ruined by having children." She looks at me sideways. "Does that surprise you? Isn't that taboo? But you are grown up now, you are married and you have two children — you are ready for the truth. You already *know* the truth."

"So it was my fault that you divorced before I was one year old?"

"Yes and no," she says. "A baby changes everything in a relationship, and in a person, too. I fought against it, went back to my wild ways. So there, it was my fault, I tried to go back to being free from husband and child."

"How could you?"

"Pride," she says. "Ego. I had no idea how hard it would be to raise a baby, which is funny because when the baby-bug bit me I didn't even want to get married, I just wanted a *baby*. But your father insisted, so we got married and then you came along. There I was, alone in a rented house only a few miles from here but several hundred miles from my parents and the house where I'd lived all my life. I had no support, and it was like all the glamour of life had just been yanked away. There was no money, we were starving students, and he helped us as much as he could but it just wasn't enough. I didn't like pregnancy, that's where the marriage tensions start, in the pregnancy, and I was counting on getting my figure back and everything going back to normal.

"Well anyway, I sinned, I failed to repent, to wear sackcloth or whatever — oops, there's my Pride again — and then I returned to my parents' house just long enough to find my next husband. Being a single mom wasn't much fun either, all my pre-marriage fantasies aside. The second marriage lasted years and I thought that maybe I'd settled down . . . well, anyway, you're a better mom than I, Gunga Din." She laughs. "What, you're the only one who gets to make puns?"

"I'm surprised at you."

"Ah, and I'm surprised at you," she says. "When I put aside my Pride, my ideas of what I wanted you to be, then I can see what you are doing, what you have already done, and I see it not as criticism of me but as expressions of your own self, and then I am happy for you and proud of you."

"That Pride again."

"Yes, but it isn't Self-Pride," she says. "Well, not exactly, at least . . . a certain amount of reflected Self-Pride, since I am the mother of this admirable person."

I feel my ears grow hot.

"So how do you do it?" she asks. "Are there some little tricks to it?"

"I don't know how," I say. I think for a moment. "I go away for a weekend every month."

"Ah, 'a room of one's own,'" she says. "I didn't figure that one out until my fourth marriage. So where do you go?"

"Car camping, mainly in the Sierras."

"How wonderful! That's even better than my work shed. And when you are on your retreat do you practice an art, work with your hands?"

"No, not really," I say. "Mostly I decompress. I unwind. I allow myself to feel. It is more like a hermitage."

"Ah, meditation."

"No," I say. "Just a kind of reviving. In the first couple of years it was really hard, taking care of the baby, and I started fragmenting. I saw myself in the third person. I spun off imaginary friends to advise me." Her eyes dart over my shoulder and then away again. "I had the desire to be more like a machine, and I envisioned myself with this protruding thing on my chest, above my heart —"

"A breast," she says.

"No, a control panel," I say, fighting against her hermetic symbolism. "With gauges showing heart, brain, nerves, and all of the senses, with knobs to control everything. So if I couldn't take her crying any more I could just turn my hearing down; if I found myself getting angry I could turn my heart down and lower my nerves. I started to actually do it — not that I would turn imaginary knobs on my chest, but I would imagine doing it."

"Did it work?"

"Yes, I think so," I say. "A little."

"Good for you," she says. "A kind of creative imagery, based on robots, leading to body control. But why don't you just buy or rent a nannybot?"

"They are still too expensive," I say. "And they still are not as good as you would like them to be."

"Ah, so the 'nannybot for the masses' remains only a dream," she says. "Well that explains a lot. Here you are, trying to become the robot I was dreaming of having."

"But I wasn't being a robot, I was being a cyborg," I say. "Part human, part machine. An explorer going into unknown space."

"As a child you always wanted to be an astronaut," she says.

"Yes, that's right! And those stories, all these pieces came bubbling up in me. The camping was the only place where I could feel human again, the only time when I could allow myself to feel anything at all. I was a space pioneer, I had all these secret powers, but on the outside I just looked like something strangely old-fashioned and goofy. A new Don Quixote, an odd Milkman."

"Well, I'm afraid I must be going now," she says, rising from the chair. As I lead her toward the door she asks, "Tell me, did you ever stop sleepwalking?"

"Huh? Sure, that was ages ago. The last time, I was a teenager."

"The beach house," she says with a faraway look.

"Yeah, that's right," I say. "You'd beaten me at chess the afternoon before, so I got up in the middle of the night and started walking to the market to get you something you needed right away."

"You locked yourself out."

"I didn't wake up until I opened the front gate."

"The way you knocked at the door until I came to let you in!" She laughs. "Tell me again what it looks like, feels like, when you are sleep walking?"

"Sometimes I don't remember anything. Other times it is like watching a movie of myself, so I don't really feel anything."

"Stay away from water, Jason," she says. She kisses my cheek. "You know how I worry."

When I open the front door for her the afternoon sunlight streams in, just like that dream before, and suddenly she isn't there anymore.

Did you see that? She saw you.

Yeah, sure, her not wanting to see the kids can be taken in that bad way, but you know what? I'm sick of everything revolving around them and I'm happier that she gave me all of the attention.

That's true, but she held back. She never said anything—

Can you hear the howls? No, behind you, on your side. Like the Furies. She wants to slap me? A few of them. "Big boys don't whine," is that . . . ?

You're fading out. I guess this is the end. Thank you for being there to help me at each stage — I couldn't have done it without you.

Learn from my mistakes. Promise me you won't do the things I've done.

Yes, my little dream has come true — I have a house, I have atonement with my mother — but the dream was not quite right. The truth is you need a family to start a family, as paradoxical as that sounds, and if you find yourself in the common family-less condition I am in, then you must buy, beg, or borrow each element. Grandparents, uncles, aunts, cousins

MAD DOGS OF MERCURY

They hid behind the first all-terrain vehicle they found in the motor shelter. Through the open end of the hanger they could see that there was no immediate pursuit from the mine, 20 meters away. "Mack" gestured for all to de-activate their suit radios, then bumped helmets with the rearguard, "Grim" Lee, for secure communications.

"Where's the hopper?" asked Grim.

"That li'l speck in the sky, heading south," said Mack. "I wager he saw it happening — maybe they tipped him off. Listen here, I'm going to huddle with the other guys. I want you to keep lookout and talk to *la chica* on open channel. Got that?" His copper brown face radiated efficiency and control.

"Yeah."

"If you see something, just say 'Remember the hotel?' if you can."

Mack left to confer with "Dirk" and "Clay," the other two bodyguards who were white and black like salt and pepper. Grim touched helmets with Brigitta Devi, their employer's secretary.

"Ms. Devi? Let's go back to radio —"

"We must go back and get him." Her light brown eyes

59

wide with fear, then steeling with defiant resolve; her skin the color of milk tea.

"Go to radio," said Grim, "but don't talk about what we are doing."

"What else are we going to talk about, the weather?"

"Sure, if you like."

"We must get him," Brigitta said. "It's in your contract." She held up her metal attaché case and shook it.

"Your boss — our boss, he's dead," Grim said. "He died instantly or within a few seconds. Now stay here, please — I have to go on sentry."

Grim left the huddle, turned on his radio. He drew his submachine gun from its holster and turned off the safety, one of the oversized vac-duty knobs that made the weapon look like a toy. He moved to the shelter entrance where he could watch both the treacherous mine and the dirt mound of the subterranean living quarters beyond it. He briefly surveyed the surrounding terrain of Beethoven Crater, a landscape that boasted all the shades of ash and burnt toast out to a horizon that was too close at only two kilometers away. Behind the horizon to the south rose the Sayat Nova Crater's rim, a dark cloud mesa 300 kilometers away. Toward that their suborbital hopper raced, a small dot getting smaller, brightly lit by the morning sunlight. It was hard to believe that there was any future on Mercury, even before this fiasco.

"You talk like a person who comes from Ophir," said Brigitta over the radio. "And you present yourself as ex-military. Did you fight the hominids in Africa?"

"Yeah."

"Which side?"

"A few."

"I'm guessing it didn't go well for you," said Brigitta.

"I'm alive."

"On Mercury."

"True," said Grim. "And Mercury is a step down for me but a step up for you."

"That's right, you military-class Ophirites have some strange attitudes about women. Are you still a virgin?"

"This isn't a good time for propositions," Grim said, his pale cheeks burning. "Maybe later."

"*Shabash*," she said, without enthusiasm. "Well, how about this weather? I'm reading an excess of thirty degrees in the shade. So how's the heat in the sunshine, Mr. *Forming*?"

"Call me Lee," he growled, irritated that she knew his real surname. "It's about a hundred." Grim glanced back and saw the huddle break, with each man moving to a different vehicle.

"How much can these suits take, anyway?" asked Brigitta.

The big sun had been slowly sinking in the east for five e-days but the temperature continued to rise at one degree per hour.

"They're rated for 120 —"

"Five man there behind car, please listen," said an almost human voice. "Here affair no against five man there behind car. Forty work peasant from Beethoven give five man free travel, no trouble. Call taxi, take to spaceport. Please drop there four gun. Come slow. Give silver luggage to work peasant."

"What sort of gibberish was that?" said Brigitta.

"That was Basic, ma'am, spoken by a hominid," said Grim.

"Darvin save us!" gasped Brigitta. "Is this a troglodyte uprising? What did it say?"

"He said they mean us no harm, but he did point out that we are outnumbered by as much as eight to one. So they want us to drop our weapons here and hand over your attaché case."

"Maybe we should?" said Brigitta, emphatically shaking her head. Everyone remembered the atrocities in Africa: surrender was unthinkable.

"He sounded like a hablis, or maybe a robust — the

robusts are bad with numbers," said Grim. "Forty means 'many' to them. Where are the humans? Weren't there supposed to be humans here?"

"This camp is supposed to have a couple of human supervisors, a half dozen or so hablis foremen, and a few dozen robusts to do the heavy labor," said Brigitta. "So are the humans dead, or are they hostages . . . or are they in on it?"

"They are usually in on it. Hey — *Remember the hotel?*"

"Huh?" said Brigitta, genuinely puzzled. "Sure, we were there only four hours ago. Of course I *remember the hotel!*"

They played at small talk for a minute until Dirk appeared, motioning Grim into a helmet huddle.

"What ya got, mate?"

"Movement over by the mine," said Grim. "Looks like they're getting some heavy equipment ready."

"Too late for them," said Dirk. "We're choofing off. Lucky bastard, babysitting the sheila." A lecherous grin split his pale face. "Next time we trade jobs, okay?" Brigitta added her helmet to the huddle and Dirk got to the point. "Here's the deal — we're taking the best car available, and we're driving out of here."

"How far?" said Grim. "Back to Sayat Nova?"

"Not so far, at first," said Dirk. "We just have to choof off this hot spot and find out if the trog uprising is insular or widespread."

"What about the case?" said Grim. "They want it."

"Pardon my asking, ma'am, but what's in it?"

"Papers," said Brigitta. "Important papers."

"Just paper?" said Dirk. "Maybe we should let 'em have it."

"A half-million in Mercury dollars."

Dirk gave a toneless whistle.

"Each one worth a hy-mark, right?" said Grim. "No wonder they want it."

"Divided by five is a hundred-thou each," said Dirk. "That's good dosh. Unless you have to return it — are you, ah, employed by the corporation, Brigitta?"

"Not me," she said. "My *pukka* employer was just killed in a booby-trap. But face it, they were worth a hy-mark each ten minutes ago, now it's probably less."

"It's ours, whatever it's worth," said Dirk. "We'll leave the decoy case, buy us some time."

The four ATVs were a standard police/paramilitary model used on Luna and Mars — the laser cannon presumably had some mining applications here on Mercury. Each had a name in bold stenciled letters: *Black Lion*, *White Lion*, *Red Lion*, and the one they chose, the *Green Lion*. It took a long three minutes for them to cycle through its tiny airlock one at a time. Grim was still in the airlock when the ATV lurched into motion. It left the shelter following the dirt track north, but when the trail bent to the northwest the *Green Lion* went off-road, bearing north.

The vehicle's interior already seemed cluttered and crowded to Grim, despite the fact it could carry twice as many people in a pinch. Mack was driving, the engine compartment to his left; the others sat on seats in the back. Two pressure hatches in the roof and a toilet in the corner next to the back door completed the picture.

"I sure wish we could mess up the other crawlers before we go," said Clay to Dirk, who was eyeing Brigitta. She sat with the attaché case primly on her thighs.

"Git up here, Grim," said Mack after Grim took his helmet off. "Git on the radio and tell those baddies goodbye. Then look around and tell us if this situation is just Beethoven or the whole South."

"Right, Mack." The communication station was in the front and center, behind the engine compartment, against the airlock wall, and below the laser turret. He pulled down the seat, sat down, and put on the headset.

"Hello, peasant worker. Here be five man." He repeated himself a few times before receiving an answer.

"Hello five man. Here be peasant worker. Bad go, bad bad. Sunrise plus twelve e-day come quick. Come tomorrow. Bad bad burn time. Five friend come back quick. Eat sleep play."

Grim laughed off-mike. "They've changed their tune. Now they call us friends and invite us to stay through siesta."

"Please have silver luggage," he said on the radio. "Five man go far distance. Goodbye."

Grim switched off the microphone and went hunting across the radio spectrum.

"Find any news?" asked Mack.

"Sounds like Sayat Nova and Chao Meng Fu have fallen," said Grim. The southern route was blocked, the south polar spaceport was closed. "But a camp called Far Nuff over at Mark Twain says they're loyal. That's north of here, I think."

"Clay, check the map for Mark Twain," said Mack. "Dirk, what's our inventory look like?"

"We've got nineteen meals," said Dirk, working his way forward.

"Four meals each," said Grim.

"About that, yeh," said Dirk. "And three of these." He held up a rocket.

"What is it?" said Mack. "I can't see back there."

"Signal flare," said Brigitta. "They fire one up to mark a mining claim."

"Looks like an anti-tank missile," said Grim.

"I found Mark Twain," said Clay. "Northwest of here, 'bout six hundred klicks."

"Okay." Stopping the ATV, Mac twisted around in his seat. "We're three klicks out, should be over the horizon from the mine. Clay, you do gunnery?"

"Nah, that's Dirk," Clay said.

"Dirk, git up in the turret, watch back for followers."

"Yeh."

"We need to cross the equator," said Mack. "Where's the nearest science outpost at?"

"That would be . . . Lysippus, straight north, 820

klicks."

Mack looked at the instrument panel. "Nah, we can't make it," he said.

"That would explain why there's no road here," said Brigitta.

Mack whipped around to look at her. "Say, *Bridge*, can you drive an ATV?"

"No," she said, stiffening.

"You'll get a chance to learn real quick."

"The road must go to Mark Twain," said Grim.

"I sure hope so," said Mack, breaking his stare. "How far from Twain to Lysippus?"

"Six hundred klicks."

"We can't call Lysippus — everybody will hear their answer, figure out our plan." Mack pivoted the vehicle west and started forward toward the northwest trail. "Lady, gentlemen, we are going to make a Warm Pole crossing. First stop, Mark Twain crater."

•

Grim was driving six hours later. Behind him, Clay said, "Hey, I going to the can."

"Okay."

Mack and Dirk were sleeping in hammocks, Clay was on radio, and Brigitta was on watch in the turret. Clay took off his vac suit and stretched.

"Hey, Brigitta," he said. To Grim he said, "Ah hell, she's napping! Wake up, Bridge!"

"Huh? What?"

"Stay alert!" He punched her leg and went to the toilet.

"All right, all right," muttered Brigitta.

Grim focused on the dirt track in front, as he had been doing for two hours. He had no training so he did not drive at top speed across the plain, but the massif of Beethoven's rim was only a couple hours away and Mack would take over again there.

"Hey!" Brigitta shouted.

An explosion slapped the ATV. The air was storming out as Grim pulled *Green Lion* to a halt and put on his helmet. Climbing out of his seat he saw Mack and Dirk putting helmets on, but there was stunned Clay, a suitless black man in near vacuum.

He's dead, thought Grim, writing him off. As he pulled Brigitta down from the turret and helped her clamp her helmet, he saw Clay leaping for the airlock. Grim readied his submachine gun while Clay got into the airlock and closed the door.

The cabin was in vacuum so the back door opened easily for the habilis who came in pistol-first. The pistol spat fire and Dirk went down, felled like a tree. Mack fired his revolver and the worker dropped out of the doorway.

Mack crouched in the doorway and fired down to the left. Stepping over Dirk, Grim moved behind Mack and saw five figures outside, two running to the ATV parked beside *Green Lion*. Undistracted by the bullets that pocked into the sides around him, Grim sprayed lead at the nearest carbineer's feet. The heavy recoil in the light gravity shoved Grim back and lifted the bullet-spray onto the target. The hominid fell in the sudden cloud of dust that sprouted around him. The others began running away, kicking up their own dust clouds.

Mack got down to the ground. The other ATV, the *Black Lion*, made a U-turn and accelerated back along the dirt road. Grim fired a burst at the retreating open back door as the last desperate worker scrambled in. Then the ATV was moving away at top speed, a tail of dust behind it.

Grim looked at the back of his own ATV and saw the breach, a laser blast that came in by the toilet. He checked Dirk, finding him dead with a shattered helmet. Mack checked that the condensing cylinder on the rear-mounted exhaust had not been hit. They could not afford to lose any of their precious water.

Without much hope Grim went inside and pounded on the airlock door. He felt the vibration of three knocks in response. Clay was alive in there!

Mack came in. Grim pointed to the airlock and gave a thumbs up. Mack gestured to his wrist, signifying time: *how quickly can we patch and repressurize, and can Clay last that long with a closet of air?*

Grim kept a watch outside for the thirty minutes it took Mack and Brigitta to seal the hole. He helped Brigitta lash the corpses to the roof as the cabin was repressurized. In silence they watched the south.

"Grim, come in through the airlock," said Mack, breaking radio silence. "Bridge, you wait until called."

In the airlock Grim saw some blood on the wall. When he entered the cabin he was relieved to see Clay sitting up with a bandage on his shoulder.

"I thought you were dead!" he said the moment he shucked his helmet.

"Me too," said Clay.

"Your shoulder?"

"Just some slivers." Clay shrugged. "It's nothin'."

"Yeah," said Mack, "but Dirk is dead. We have a problem — Bridge is not keeping up her end. She was sleeping, for Darvin's sake!"

"It's my fault," said Clay. "I should've kept an eye on her."

"She nearly got us all killed."

"What do you want to do, leave her out there?" said Grim.

"No, course not," said Mack. "But I don't want to reward the weak link, neither. I don't want to give her a portion of the *lechuga* from the partner she just killed!"

"So she gets her one-fifth and we divide Dirk's three ways?" said Clay.

"Or she gets *nada* and we split the whole thing three ways," said Mack.

Grim looked at Clay, who rolled his eyes and looked at

Mack.

"Look here," said Mack. "If either one or both of you want to give her part of your share once we get out of this mess, that's your business. But I'm not about to reward such a royal screw-up."

Mack called her in. When she cycled through they saw she had taken the hominid's carbine. She endured Mack's tongue-lashing; she accepted the financial penalty without comment; she apologized for falling asleep on watch.

•

Seventeen hours later the *Green Lion* rolled up to camp Far Nuff at Mark Twain crater. Grim's suit started warning him about the heat the moment he stepped out.

Grim, Mack, and Brigitta went through the large airlock to the camp's living area, leaving Clay to guard the ATV. They caused a commotion among the hominids in the rough-hewn tunnels, and had to wait while a rex went off to find a human.

"Gum?" said a 2 meter tall robust, moving in close, his red ape fur making him seem like a shaggy wall. "Candy?" His big jaw was frightening, even though it signaled his vegetarian diet.

"No, no," said Grim.

"No bother guest," said a habilis who was 50 centimeters smaller. "No gum, no candy. Ed go bed." This one was small and dark haired, but still quite stocky.

"What's that grassy smell?" said Brigitta.

"That's the vegan vat," said Mack.

One of the robusts broke wind. Two others followed suit.

Grim laughed. "Hey, it's just like that cartoon, you know? 'Handy and Stinky'?"

The robusts were laughing, too, even though they could not follow the language. They knew the humor of it.

"The little bossy one and the big gas bag!" shrieked

Brigitta.

The homo erectus came back with a Chinese man who said, "I'm Chin. You must be the desperados from Beethoven."

"Well . . . "

"Come to my office, this way. Please excuse the mess."

At the office Chin dismissed the curious robusts who had followed.

"I don't want any trouble," he said the moment the door was sealed. "My hominids don't know about the uprising and I don't want them to. Beethoven is telling one and all that you stole *Green Lion* and some other stuff." He looked at the attaché case that Grim held. "They didn't say exactly what and I don't want to know. They're coming and they'll be here within two to six hours. You can't stay here — you can't even take a shower here."

"We need to buy some hydrogen," said Mack. "Tank's close to empty."

"All righty, we might be able to do that." Chin sat down and started flicking at an abacus. "You are going to trade in your water, I assume?"

"Yes."

"You have it all?"

"Yes."

"Good." He flicked at the beads. "I heard there was a fight with a blowout — thought you might've lost some." He wrote something on a slip of paper. "Here is the price," he said, handing it to Mack.

Mack looked at it, handed it to Grim.

"Is that in Mercury dollars?" asked Grim as Brigitta glanced at the price.

"Darvin, no!" said Chin. "That's in hy-marks. In unsettled times like these I must insist on trading in more stable currencies."

"But you will give change in Mercury dollars," said Brigitta.

"Naturally," said Chin, nodding his head solemnly.

"I imagine you would give a considerable discount for deu-marks," said Brigitta.

"Now wait —" started Mack.

"Yes, yes I would," said Chin, caught off-balance and rushing in. He scribbled another figure, handing it to Mack.

Glancing at the new price, Brigitta took a breath and let it out with a "Hmmm." She looked directly at Chin. "I was thinking the discount would be twice as much."

Chin rolled his eyes, scribbled again, handed the slip to Brigitta.

Brigitta's nose twitched. "All right," she said. "But this is just for fuel. We need food and supplies, ammunition for guns and the laser cannon, as well as things we don't even know we need for this dangerous drive. I'd like a heavy duty vac suit, myself."

"I don't have any," Chin said sadly, but then he snapped his fingers and grinned. "Reflective tarp! At least one to tie on the roof of the car, to reduce the life support drain, and another one to make shade if you have to go outside . . ."

When all the haggling was done, Brigitta paid in crisp deuterium-based cash from her own wallet. Chin gave her change in Mercury dollars.

"Now you can tell me what this stuff is worth off-planet," said Brigitta, waving a small fan of the dollars Chin had given her. "No hard feelings, I promise."

"I'm not sure," Chin admitted. "Between a third and a fifth, I think."

Chin accompanied the visitors outside with a work party of robusts. He found out about the corpses on the roof and offered to give them burial but Mack refused.

"The one is our friend," he said. "The rest are evidence."

Once the purchases were cycled through the airlock and the reflective tarp was in place on the roof, it was time to go.

"There's the trail to Lysippus," said Chin, pointing out the long line stretching northeast. "Keep on the main trail. Avoid the minor trails — there are a few shortcuts but most are dead ends. A clever driver could find a shady spot a few kilometers away and nap for a few hours, keeping an eye on the camp here and an ear on the radio."

"Thanks, Mr. Chin." Mack offered his hand.

"Problem is, you are racing the heat," Chin continued as he shook hands. "Close to the temperature limit of your suits now."

Mack cycled through. Chin shook hands with Brigitta. "Darvin help you if you have a breakdown and have to go outside. If you use the tarp to make shade, remember it will still take a while for the ground to cool off, and heat will continue to come in from beyond the shadow."

Brigitta cycled through. Chin shook hands with Grim. "It is a mad dog thing, a mad dog run. Nobody goes out in the Mercury sunlight after e-day eleven. Good luck to you all."

•

Twelve hours later the *Green Lion* crossed the point of no return.

"We can't drive back now, there's not enough fuel," said Mack. "If we get in a fight or a breakdown and we lose fuel, we're dead. If we get holed in a fight, that isn't so bad — we're wearing helmets from here on out. But if we lose fuel then we got to get more fuel from the other guy, we have to go out there in a rush. Bridge stays here to guard the case. The rest of us will each carry a signal rocket to punch a hole in the other car's cabin."

The trail had snaked around a pocked plain of small craters for some time when Clay said, "Uh-oh. Got somethin'. Car-to-suit chatter."

"Must be close," said Mack, driving again. "Chaz damn it!"

The *Green Lion* continued on, driving along the base of a small escarpment, the cliff and its shade to the right. Through the turret window Grim saw the *Red Lion* nosing out of a break in the cliff just as the *Green Lion* passed, a near collision.

"Here they are, on the right!" shouted Grim.

Mack accelerated the *Green Lion* away, putting 50 meters between the two vehicles. Bringing the laser cannon to bear, Grim saw that the *Red Lion* had a strange structure on its roof behind the turret, something like an open-sided tent made of reflective tarp. Several figures were riding in the shade there, and something shot past Grim's head, trailing smoke and sparks from out of that shadowy shelter.

Grim fired the cannon. Another rocket from the *Red Lion* roof party leapt forward, coming low, and hit the *Green Lion* with two separate thuds. The breached ATV came to a limping halt, its motor slagged, its atmosphere rushing out a new wound in its side.

Grim jumped down and went into a helmet huddle with Mack and Clay, catching the end of their conversation: "— remember, we want a breach only," said Mack.

"Right," said Clay.

"Grim, we gotta take that car intact," said Mack. "Clay's on rocket, we're supporting him. Let's go!"

There was no time to tell Brigitta anything. They went out through the two opened doors of the airlock.

When Grim stepped down onto the dirt his suit warned him about the heat. He knew the suit's shoes could only endure a few minutes of such high temperature but that would be enough time, either way. Already it was like walking on hot coals. Contact with a less insulated part of the suit would cause immediate blowout — a fall would be fatal. *Live forever or die today,* he thought.

Mack waved and started forward. Grim followed him around the ATV's rear corner. The *Red Lion* had stopped

20 meters away. A worker stood in the shade of the roof shelter, aiming a carbine at them; a second completed his jump down to the pair already on the ground, one of whom had a laser carbine.

Clay launched his rocket at the ATV's broad side. It narrowly missed, but spooked the driver. Clay went down to the laser carbine. Grim moved to target the laser man but he had already fallen so he turned and peppered the next one with fire, leaning into the recoil from his submachine gun fire. The falling hominid's rifle exploded when it hit the ground, its ammunition spontaneously combusting in the heat.

The *Red Lion* began moving away. Mack and Grim ran after it, ignoring the last hominid on the ground. Grim heard a strange crackling sound that was his lower suit frying like bacon on a hot skillet.

Sweat was pouring down his face. He saw Mack take a running jump and quickly did the same himself. In the one-third gravity the two men soared four meters up. It was almost enough to reach the *Red Lion* but Grim could see that he would not make it, and failure meant death. *I need a booster,* he thought.

Instinctively he pointed his gun down and back, then fired off a burst that pushed him up. Mack descended toward the ground but Grim flew awkwardly, fighting against a twist and a tumble. He landed on the roof where his boots slipped for an instant before finding solid purchase.

The lone roof-rider had moved away during Grim's gun-assisted leap, but now he moved in close, using his carbine as a cudgel. It was too close for the submachine gun so Grim responded in kind, using it as a club. He discovered that his molten boots were stuck to the cold roof.

The *Red Lion* continued at speed, swerving and bumping over the rough terrain as the two spacemen went at it like cavemen. Neither could land a solid blow through the tough armor of their suits, but time was on the side of the workers.

With his sixth attempt Grim pounded his opponent with a hard hit that sent him down to the roof.

Grim readied his flare rocket. The ATV began swerving violently, causing his downed opponent to roll off to certain death on the hot ground. Grim fell back. One of his boots became unstuck but the left one held. He rose to standing and the tarp in front of him was blasted away by a pulse from the turret to his left.

Grim thought of launching his one rocket at the turret: he could see the helmet-less man's face in the window slit, but the risk of failure was too great. Instead he fired it at the back rear of the roof.

He expected it to neatly punch through the roof and rear, causing a very sudden decompression through two holes. But his heart sank as the flare rocket ricocheted off the roof and accelerated into the sky, the distance having proved to be too short for the missile to get enough speed.

Grim readied his gun to blast at the turret glass, but suddenly the ATV came to a hard stop. Grim's anchor boot came lose, wrenching his ankle. As he slid along the roof he caught the hatch wheel. Looking up toward the back he saw a blowing spout of cabin confetti, proof that the rocket dent had opened into a small hole after all.

The hatch sensor knew that the cabin was depressurized so it let him in. Grim dropped down with gun ready. He found the two men preoccupied with putting on their helmets.

"Drive back or I'll kill you," Grim said over the radio.

The men complied.

"Come in *Green Lion*, this is Grim," he said over the ATV radio as they came within visual range. "Come in Mack, Brigitta."

They could all be dead, he thought. *Then what? Grab the money and kill —*

"Hey Grim, what's the score?" crackled Mack's voice.

"Mack, I'm bringing them back."

"Chaz Darvin, you did it!" said Mack. "I was afraid you might have bad news."

"How're things over there?"

"We got a prisoner and Bridge saved Clay from the fire, if you can believe it."

Grim thought about the prisoner dilemma for the rest of the ride. *Don't want to kill them, don't want to guard them, and don't want to leave them . . .*

•

Ten hours later *Red Lion* pulled into Lysippus base with three prisoners and several corpses riding on the roof beneath a restored tarp shelter. From there the living and the dead took a hopper flight to Desprez Crater near the north pole.

•

"It's Clay, the man who wouldn't die," said Grim.

"Hey Grim, I haven't seen you in a few," said Clay. "Find what you were lookin' for?"

"Yeah."

"All right," said Clay after waiting a beat for more information. "Don't forget the flight's going out tomorrow."

"I'm not going. I sold my ticket."

"Huh? What'd you say?"

"I needed the money."

"On top of the cash?"

"Yeah," said Grim. "Now I'm broke."

"Huh. I thought *I* was spendin' a lot, giving half of mine to Brigitta."

"Your life is worth it."

"That's true, that's true," said Clay. "So what's next for you?"

"I dunno," said Grim. "Find a job around here."

"No particular hurry?"

"Nah."

"You don't seem like a gambler or an addict, but I sure didn't peg you for a *philosopher*."

Grim shrugged.

"So you found a *stone* here?"

"Yeah."

"And now you're good for another year — aren't you kinda young for this? Those people are all over thirty."

"You're never too young to stop aging."

"I don't know . . . "

"That's my reason for doing what I do," said Grim Lee. "I have this saying, 'Live forever or die today.'"

"Grim Lee, the man who wouldn't age," said Clay, laughing. "I guess we're more alike than I thought. I'll see you around, Mr. Lee."

"I hope so, Clay," said Grim as they shook hands. "And it's Forming, but you can call me Lee."

HARDBOILED PROUST

"There is the sordid Balbec of reality here, all around us, and the Balbec of dream which is struggling to be born" — Mr. Milieu, Director of Background Characters.

I couldn't sleep because my body was still on California time, meaning I was nine hours off. After tossing and turning most of the night, I finally gave up, put on my new 19th-century clothes, and left my hotel room. I went down the stairs that circled the off-duty lift cage, then walked through the marble forest of the Grand Hotel until I found myself out on the promenade of Proust's Balbec.

To the north was the star-lit ocean. To the west a man sprawled on a bench next to the bandstand, a drunk sleeping it off. The place was like a movie studio's back lot when nothing was being filmed.

I went east, with shuttered kiosks on my right and beach tents on my left. About three hundred yards later, I turned and came back through the deserted araby.

As I neared the drunkard, the shadows around him shifted so that for an instant I thought he sat bolt upright, then I realized there was a small person bending over him, hands moving across his body.

I hurried forward. The small figure jerked in surprise and snatched up a golf club resting against the bench. It was a teenage girl with a dark ponytail wearing a boyishly Victorian athletic suit, with something like a baseball helmet, a dark jacket, and a pair of light pants.

"What's going on?" I asked her.

"Nothing," she said defiantly, but her body language told me she was just this side of running away. "Only checking to see if he's all right."

"Sleeping it off, huh?" I figured that she'd been rolling the drunk, so I poked him. "Hey, wake up."

I took his hand and dropped it — it was icy cold.

"He's dead!"

"I was afraid of that," she said.

"Go get the police," I said. "I'll wait here."

She darted off and soon was out of sight behind the looming hotel.

"Good evening," said a deep, gravelly voice behind me.

I turned to see a portly man strolling toward me on silent feet. His pale hand held a cigar near his mouth. He was strangely dark and lumpy.

"Hello," I said. "I found this dead man here, sent the girl to get the police."

I could see that the smoker was wearing a suit of tires from head to toe — a walking advertisement.

"You look like you could use a drink," he said. He handed me a flask.

"Thanks," I said. I drank and tasted licorice.

"You said there was a filly?" he said as he took back the flask.

"Yeah. She had a hat like a baseball helmet."

"A polo cap?"

"Maybe. Yeah, I guess so."

He rumbled a thoughtful hum.

"She will not go to the police, that one." He drew on the cigar so the tip glowed like a taillight.

"You sure?"

He blew out a cloud of smoke. "But yes, certainly."

"Will you go to the police?"

He laughed. "No, but I will guard and you can go."

"But I just got here last night," I said. "I don't know my way around town."

"Have them telephone from the lobby."

I left him and did just that.

When I came back, the tire-man was gone.

Dawn was breaking when the gendarme showed up and asked to see my passport.

"Tourist?" he asked as he opened it up.

"No, employee," I said. "I just got here last night."

"What's your job?"

"I don't know yet."

He tsked at that.

"Well, so what happened here? You called, right?"

I told him the story.

"You've been drinking," he said. "I smell it on you."

"I just had that one drink, I told you."

"Yes, I know," he said. "From that hallucination."

He felt the corpse's hand, then searched for identity papers, tsking when he found nothing.

"He looks like a banker," he said. "A word of advice, *mon ami* — stay away from poseurs and hallucinations. We are milieus, you and I — we will never be majors or minors, but we are the solid muscles that keep this theme zone moving. We are low men on the pole totem, but lower still are poseurs and hallucinations — they are things in the soil, maggots and worms. Comprehend?"

I didn't get it completely, but I nodded.

"Good. And if you see that poseur Albertine again, let us know. We want to question her."

"You think she killed him? The body was cold."

The gendarme shrugged. "Criminals often come back to the scene of a crime."

•

I slept until eleven o'clock. When I looked out my window I saw the promenade alive with strollers in period clothing — what had seemed like a back-lot movie set in the darkness was now a living town. Proust had visited Balbec a few times around 1900, and so the place had been remade in the fashion of that era, a monument to time recaptured.

Finding myself alone in the elevator with the liftboy, I showed him my invitation card as introduction.

"Oh, I thought you were a tourist," he said, relaxing somewhat by pushing his cap back. He looked to be twenty years old, or thereabouts. His olive jacket had a Prussian collar and three lines of brass buttons down his chest. "Did you hear? They found a body on the beach last night."

"Yeah."

"It was Evan Seward, from the bank."

"Evan Seward?"

"Yeah," said Lift. "He was a milieu homie but lately he'd been seen around with Albertine — farting higher than his ass, and maybe Octave objected. My money's on Octave."

"Uh huh, so now maybe you can tell me about this place," I said. "I'm here. Now what do I do?"

"You have to see your director."

"My director?"

"Mr. Milieu," he said. "Director of Background Characters. His office is in the basement."

"And what will he do for me?"

"Interview, audition, advise — whatever. He's the one who will assign you your place in Balbec." He got a sly look. "Did you bring any contraband?"

"Like what?"

"Anything. I could use a coke."

"No, nothing. Sorry. So anyway, this director will give me my job placement — say as an elevator operator at the Grand Hotel."

He hooted. "In your dreams! I'm a minor character, different director. You're far too old to be a liftboy — I'm nearly too old myself, expect to be transferred any day now."

"So as a minor character you are a step above the background characters."

His surprised look told me how incredibly stupid I seemed, as if I had neglected to do even the slightest bit of homework and was now asking him for crib notes on my way to the final exam.

"Well, in theory, yes," he said. "Because the role comes under greater scrutiny — not nearly as much as the major league, but still a lot more than the grounders. No offense."

I stepped out of the lift on the ground floor and asked a last question. "So who's watching?"

"Tourists, theme police, you know," he said as he closed the outer door of metal lattice. "But the toughest audience is always your peers, members of the majors and the minors . . . and the milieus, I suppose."

•

The milieu-king of Balbec was propped up in bed when his secretary brought me into the cork-lined bedroom.

He had a thick mustache and a thin beard of three-days' growth. It was obvious that his bed was also his desk and office: one rattan nightstand was piled with books and papers, the other had all of this and an antique telephone. Small scraps of paper were pinned to the walls.

"Yes?" he said, looking up from a pile of scribbled notes.

I handed him the paper. He asked for my passport so I gave it to him. He glanced at the passport photo, looked at me, then set it down and read the full text of the paper, starting with *As you undoubtedly know, your surname is not at all common — in fact, it is rare* and ending with *Come home to*

Balbec, where there is always a place for you.

"So," he said, and then he looked up from the page. "You would like to apply for a position here?"

"I thought I was being invited."

"Many are called, few are chosen. Have you read The Book?"

I admitted I had not read *Remembrance of Things Past*. He sighed.

"Very few have, it seems," said Mr. Milieu. "Ever played the game version? Seen the movie?"

"No and no."

"Ah. Not even curious?"

"Well, now that I know that my name is in there somewhere, yeah, I'm mildly curious. Still — it is a big book."

"Yes, yes it is," said Milieu, steeping his fingers. "And it gets bigger, like a living thing. Do you know the story of its composition? No, of course you don't, forgive me. Here is the short of it: the text that was cobbled together and published was corrupt. The first reconstruction came a generation later, and our Holographic Society is engaged in the process of the ultimate reconstruction."

"This is a book," I said. "So everybody in The Book will be found in this town — only this town?"

"No, we have sister sites in Paris, and the two Combrays. Eventually we will control the entire Coast of Flowers, but there are still a few details to work out. In any event, it is more than just this town."

"More than just Bloomsday in Dublin."

"Exactly," said Milieu with a big smile. "They have one day a year to re-enact their book. So mechanical — like a train schedule: this actor moves here at such and such a time, this actress does this, et cetera. A clockwork one-day carnival.

"What we aim for is a living, breathing, physical manifestation of a vision. An organic symphony taking into account the rhythms of the seasons and the unscripted nature of human life."

"It all sounds pretty wonderful, but where do I fit in?"

"It will take a few days to determine that," said Milieu. "I lost my agent, after only two months. He was killed."

"Evan Seward."

"Yes, that's right."

"I knew an Evan Seward years ago," I said. "We worked together on the Joyce Project before the IPO."

"That's the same one," Milieu said, wiping his nose with a tissue. "What a coincidence! Unless, no . . . wait." He rummaged through the papers for a while.

"Ah, yes, here it is!" he said, drawing forth a scrap. "He was your sponsor — he was the one who sent for you." He read the note. "So you're a substanciator, a sort of text-detective like Evan, is that right?"

"Yeah."

"What did you do at Joyce Project?" he asked.

"Detail work with an eye to historical accuracy."

"Such as . . . ?"

"Pear Soap, composition thereof. Potted meat products. Guinness Stout, bottling technology."

"I see." He blew his nose. "You left under a cloud, if I remember correctly?"

"We both did, yes."

"What was it about? Evan never told me."

"Creative differences," I said. "Management had become top heavy, and they were talking philosophy all the time. They had drifted away from the text."

"Ever work on the census? The doomsday book for 1904 Dublin?"

"A little," I said. "Most of that was already done by that point."

"Evan was working on a census," said Milieu. "Balbec has expanded rapidly and we don't have accurate numbers or names. Can you use a gun?"

"Sure. Comes with the job." That process by which culture custodians had become night watchmen of content.

"I'll hire you directly."

"Okay, but I've got to tell you up front, I can't speak French."

He looked at me with a pained expression and asked, "But what are you speaking now?"

"English."

"A debased form of Parisian," he said, waving his hand. "Most suitable for this region of Normandy."

•

When I left my new boss a few minutes later, I went straight to the lobby counter. Manager Malaprop was leading a fashionable woman toward the dining hall, so I asked Squinty the page if he knew an Octave.

"But of course," said Squinty. "He's a homie well known. A minor."

"Where could I find him?"

"Usually at the hippodrome, but for the lunch right now he is here."

I went into the dining hall for my first meal of the day. The windows were big, going down to the floor, giving a view of the sea with the promenade and the bandstand in the foreground. It felt like I was inside an aquarium, on display for the strollers.

Before I ordered I asked the waiter Aimé to indicate which diner was Octave. He did, directing my gaze to a man just leaving his table.

Octave was a rakish young man of lean build. He wore a bow tie and a yellow suit. His hair was crimped and oiled; his face was clean-shaven.

I chatted with Amié about the menu for a minute or two, interrupted by a bang outside that sounded like a gunshot. Aimé smiled and shrugged, explaining that it was Octave's car.

As I waited for my meal I looked over the vest-pocket booklet Milieu had given me: a crib sheet for book and town, a timeframe from 1880 to 1920.

"Octave (minor): age twenty to fifty-five. Playboy, gambler . . . dissipated . . . friend of Albertine . . . "

"Albertine (major): age sixteen to twenty, hair brown, eyes brown. Central love of M. Known for her *impudent expression* and her *laughing eyes*. After her death M molests a girl with same name. His jealousy over her intimacy with Morel, Aimé, Esther, Lea, Andrée . . . "

This entry game me pause. So that girl robbing the dead milieu was a major named Albertine? The gendarme said she was Albertine after hearing my description, but he called her a poseur.

"M (major): age seventeen to fifty-one, the nameless narrator, a common Parisian who gains welcome in aristocratic circles, with seasonal vacations at the Balbec beach and the Cambray hills . . . jealousy over Albertine (see Odette/Swann) . . . "

"Liftboy (minor): age seventeen to twenty . . . go-between w/ Albertine and M . . . "

It all sounded like a soap opera to me. I flipped to the front and found Aimé, who turned out to be a minor. I tried to find my name but it wasn't in there, after all. On impulse I tried looking up the tire-man.

"(Michelin man) a.k.a. Bibendum . . . historical (1898+), but not in text . . . "

I ate my food and left Aimé a big tip.

•

Balbec (previously known as "Cabourg") is laid out like an open fan: the traffic circle in front of the Grand Hotel is the center from which a dozen streets radiate, most of them on the diagonal. The lateral cross-streets are all curves. At the base of the fan lies the Grand Hotel, at the upper edge lies City Hall.

I walked south to Delamer Avenue, a one-way street feeding the circle. As I walked along those three tree-lined blocks, full of fine French food and facing beautiful weather, the place got to me. It reminded me of Main Street at Disneyland, with that mixture of horse-drawn carriages, omnibuses, and early motorcars, but with a very important difference — Disneyland's street was a re-creation, this was real, somehow, or more real. And instead of an American friendliness, there was an essence of French style, sophistication, and class division.

Belges Boulevard had the post office, City Hall, and the police station, which is where I went. I filled out the residency form and asked for the concealed gun permit. The desk-sergeant went away for a while, then came back and led me to the Police Chief Neuman, an oily little butterball with a handlebar mustache.

"Aren't you the homie who found the body this morning?" said Neuman.

"Yes."

"And now you've got his job. Funny."

I shrugged.

"I'd like to see the body," I said.

"Again?" he grunted. "Sure. First you've got to pass your shooting test before I give you a license."

I am not good at tests, but through hard experience I've learned to give the testers what they want. This guy was out to make me look stupid, to rattle me, but I was going to play along.

We went downstairs to a basement shooting range. He grabbed three revolvers and a jar of mixed ammo from a locker, put the guns on the counter and poured out the cartridges.

"You're from California," he said. "Maybe you're a cowboy — I'll bet you're a Colt man. Am I right?"

I admitted that the first pistol I learned was a Colt single action. He insisted that I try the Spanish pistol, an Orbea Hermanos 1915 in 8mm, and he offered to loan it to me.

With a 6.5 inch barrel it was obviously too long for my

purposes, but I wasn't going to fall for that gag.

The first task was to find the right cartridge in the pile. I'm not at all metric — my usual pistol is a .40 caliber Glock automatic — but I knew that .40 caliber is around 10mm and .38 caliber is 9mm. There was nothing so familiar in this ammo pile, where "7,65mm" cartridges mixed with "8mm." I tried a few before I found the right one, and I would have loaded five more but he said one would be enough, already grinning at my greenhorn ability with archaic firearms.

I shrugged but followed instructions, closing the loading gate and spinning the cylinder around so that the cartridge was at ten o'clock. I cocked the hammer, took aim at the paper target down the gallery, and pulled the trigger. The gun clicked and my hand jerked down, expecting a recoil that didn't come. Neuman got a big laugh out of that.

I thought it was a misfire, that the bastard had given me dud ammo, but the cartridge was now at eight o'clock — the cylinder rotated counterclockwise. So that was the gag. I clicked the gun at the target several more times before it fired.

It went like that for the other pistols. Neuman wiped his eyes and signed my permit. Then he took me to the morgue.

"Is that him?"

I could now see through the disguise of Belle Époque fashion to recognize the corpse of my old friend.

"Yeah," I said. "I worked with him years ago."

"He was shot in the back," said Neuman. "With a thirty-two."

"Did he die instantly?"

Neuman shrugged. "Probably not."

"He was shot there, by the Grand Hotel?"

"Non, there's not blood enough," said Neuman. "There he was dumped. We've got statements that he was last seen out at Californie on the night of the murder."

"Californie?"

"One of the farm-restaurants," said Neuman. "Bad crowd. He was there and he got a telephone call from a dame, then he withdrew a lot of money and left in a hurry."

"It's like a bank?"

"Money laundry. We should shut it down sometime, but it would just start up again at one of the other farms."

"Any suspects?"

"Besides you?" said Neuman, twirling his mustache. "I don't know. Heard anything?"

"Something about Octave being a jealous guy."

"Yeah, I heard that one, too," he said, "but I wonder about Albertine. Sound of gunshots over by her place last night, or maybe it was a car backfiring. Looks like blood on the sidewalk."

•

Back at the Grand Hotel, Mr. Milieu showed me the gun collection. The broomhandle Mauser was tempting but bulky. I couldn't decide between the .32 caliber Browning No. 1 and the .25 caliber Browning Baby, so I took them both.

•

Proust's big book lists seventy characters for the town of Balbec, including nameless bit-parts that are technically milieus. For eight years "Balbec, Incorporated" had employed a couple thousand people to run a theme zone where the seasonal tourists swell the population to thirty thousand or more, so obviously most of the employees are milieus.

Major characters (like Albertine) are ranked above minor characters (like Liftboy and Octave); minors are ranked above listed milieus (like "Dairymaid" and "Man with Feather in Hat"). The milieus have their own elaborate ranking system comparing bits, silent-bits, walk ons, name-onlies, and I don't know what else: the big division is the few "listed" milieus and the multitude of "not-listed" milieus.

The butchers (seventeen shops), the bakers (twenty-four bakeries), the cabinet-makers (five shops); the "rachels" (twenty-three brothels), the stables (nine), the cartwrights (six shops) . . . and more, all milieus.

I needed to find another place to stay since the Grand Hotel was too pricey for me, so I killed two birds with one stone by starting my census work visiting the lesser establishments in the "fan."

I found her behind the counter of a flophouse on west Mal. Foch Avenue. She was reading a comic book that showed a polo cap-wearing girl in a gang of girls who carried golf clubs on their shoulders with thuggish menace. Naturally it was The Book in graphic novel form.

"I almost didn't recognize you without your polo cap," I said.

She started and looked up at me with eyes first wide, then narrowed with contempt.

"Save your saliva, tourist," she said. "You're too old for me — it's disgusting."

She was fifteen and I was forty. But her turning my statement into a pickup line pissed me off, so I decided to ride hard.

"What kind of filly walks the beach after midnight, rolling drunks?"

"What are you saying? It's Chinese." She looked at her comic, turning the page.

"What's your real name, 'Albertine'?"

She paled at that but then came roaring back:

"I shit on you on foot, on horseback, and in the car!"

"Listen nightwalker," I said. "Seward was murdered and you were on him like a hyena. The gendarmes are looking for you like they're going to pin the killing on you."

She glanced around furtively.

"But I don't think you did it," I said. "Tell me what happened."

Her dark eyes started to tear up.

"I was just out walking —"

"Save it," I said.

"All right," she said with a swallow. Her eyes dried up. "I'll tell you, but you're not going to believe it."

I waited.

"I got a telephone call from a strange homie, I don't know who. He called me 'Albertine' and told me to make a pick up from an old guy on the promenade. That's how it was, I swear it!"

"You have a telephone?" I asked, since they are restricted in Balbec.

"It's this one here," she said. "If it rings in the middle of the night, I have to answer it."

"So somebody else knows your secret identity?"

"A handful." She shrugged. "Maybe ten."

That threw me since I had thought it was more secret than that, a lever I could use on her. To recover I said, "How many Albertine-poseurs are there, anyway?"

"A few. Depends on who you ask."

"Huh," I said. "Because someone was telling me about how Seward had been seen around town with 'Albertine,' and maybe Octave got jealous — I thought it was you."

"Oh no, that's dead Albertine, the town slut," she said.

"How can you be so sure?"

"There's only one Albertine, *mon dieu*. Like a queen bee. She's out, too old for the job, and the director is having a hard time replacing her."

"How come?"

"Maybe it's her doing, maybe it's Octave," she said with a shrug. "Maybe both."

"And you want to be the new queen bee."

"I could do it," she said. "And better than her. She goes over the line — she's money-crazy. That's not the spirit of The Book, and it sure ain't the letter."

"Tell me about Octave."

"He's a tough homie," said the girl. "Like a gangster of the underground economy. He has a car and an entourage — they hang out at the race track."

•

I went to the telephone exchange to trace the call. Eventually they showed me the log entry: the call to the flophouse had come from the Californie, a place that had three lines (office, bar, and booth). The call had come from the booth.

I tried to trace the call to the bar that had come hours earlier, but there were too many calls to really help much.

By that point it was dinnertime. I took a hack to the Californie, out in the countryside beyond the easy reach of the theme police. On the outside it was a typical farmhouse of Normandy, with half-timbers, whitewash, and thatch. Expanded a bit, but all in the same style, so the theme police would not get them on building code violations. But once I was inside this twenty-first century speakeasy, I could hear the rock music playing — the Doors, Jefferson Airplane, and the Beach Boys. The air was thick with smoke of marijuana and tobacco, and the waiters wore blue jeans. There were a lot of tourists there, international people desperate for familiar food.

Somebody called me over — it was Liftboy and a teenage guy. They invited me to sit at their table.

"Hey, how's it going?" said Lift. "You been assigned yet?"

"Yeah, I'm working for Mr. Milieu. Doomsday book."

"Huh," said Lift. "Sounds studious."

The waiter came. The two had already ordered hamburgers, fries, and cokes. I ordered pancakes and coffee.

"This here's the new Liftboy," said Lift, introducing me to his companion. "He just got in today, so I'm showing him around a bit before I shuffle off the role and into limbo."

I said hi to the kid and asked Liftboy, "So what are your prospects? Going up, going down, or flying steady?"

"I don't know — I don't think I can go up. The major league is pretty small, pretty tight. To stay at the same level, maybe I could become Chauffeur, or a new Octave.

"But you, my boy," he said, turning to the new Liftboy. "Your future is bright and secure. Remember, you are a bisexual concerned with discretion — what you do on your own time is immaterial, but when you are on role you must be in character. Repeat after me: 'It's enough for one person to talk, word gets around, and you can't find another place anywhere.'"

The boy dutifully rattled it off.

"Good. And when Saint Loup makes his pass — mark my words, *when* Saint Loup makes his pass, you must demur this way. Quite a cock tease, really! But it is all for the best — no good comes of mixing between the majors and the minors."

"What about M?" asked the boy.

"Now you're playing coy, just for our friend here. Should M appear, he will be a young guy a few years older than you. No cock-teasing — play it straight. Give him the lay of the land, run messages for him, that sort of thing. But don't get your hopes up since he might never show up."

"Did you ever see him?" asked the boy.

"I can't really say."

"And what about Albertine?" asked the boy.

Old Liftboy looked like he had been punched in the gut. "Good question. But which Albertine? She is like a current, a wave running through us."

"There's only one Albertine, *mon dieu*," I said.

"Have you seen her yet?" Lift asked me, his eyes lighting up.

"No."

"But you've read The Book, right?"

"No," I said. "I've just heard talk that she's some kind of dame."

"She is, *mon ami*, she is," said Lift. "Let me tell you, you'll be disappointed when you first see her. 'This is the Helen of Balbec?' you will ask yourself. But then, somehow, you will fall under her spell and see that she is the center of the world. At that moment, you are caught."

"You sound . . . experienced."

"Yes."

"I hear she likes money."

"She does, but it is refreshing in a way," said Lift. "She is so open about it she puts to shame the virtuous women and the rachels as well."

"You tried hard, didn't you?"

"I took on additional jobs to afford her."

"Additional jobs?"

"Here and there," said Lift. "It's embarrassing — please don't tell anyone." He turned to his replacement, saying, "And don't let this happen to you."

"So how did it end between you and her?" I asked.

"I ran out of money."

"Just like that?"

He reddened and nodded.

"No hard feelings?"

"No," he said. "I feel like I owe her — she's a goddess. After me came Octave. Then Seward."

The pancakes were fine, the coffee was good. I called Mr. Milieu from the phone booth, just to try out the technology.

"Is the Californie really in The Book?" I asked him.

He assured me it was. He rattled off a menu that did not include cheeseburgers or onion rings.

"It seems like a gray area to me, census wise," I said.

"Just focus on the legitimate business," he said. "See no evil. Evan got on well there, you should be fine."

"Who owns the place?"

"Octave the playboy."

"Is *that* in The Book?"

"Non."

I talked to the bartender, then the manager. I got a roster of the employees, and there was a familiar name among the part-timers — Liftboy.

"I guess it is unusual for a minor to moonlight," I said.

"It's forbidden," said the manager, his pronounced Adam's apple bobbing.

"So how did Lift get on?"

"He's leaving the minors. Octave gave him a break, or maybe it was a favor for Albertine."

I asked if Lift had worked the night before; he said no. I asked if Octave had been in last night; he said no.

I went out to ask Lift a few questions but he and the boy were gone.

I talked to the bartender again and went behind the bar to try the view from there.

"You were working here last night, right?"

"Yeah."

"Was it quiet or busy?"

"It's never quiet," he said. "It was very busy."

"You got the call for Seward?"

"Yeah."

"Who was it?"

"Albertine."

"You sure?"

"Yeah."

"You got a house weapon in case of trouble?" I asked.

"Sure."

"Can I see it?"

It was a pistol hanging on a hook under the counter: a Webley .32 with the smell of recent use.

"You shoot this last night?"

"Non."

I told him I was going to borrow it for police work. He shrugged.

•

I took a hack back to town. After I dropped off the revolver at the police station I took another ride in order to
meet the "dead" Albertine, the so-called goddess.

Her place was on Foch, three blocks down from the
flophouse where filly Albertine worked. It was a two-story
building that used to have a shop on the ground floor. I
rang the bell and the door was opened by a big, square woman whose black hair was cut short. She looked like a
weightlifter in her thirties.

"Albertine?" I said, trying to keep my voice neutral.

"No," she said with a surprised little smile. "I'm Gort."

"I'd like to see Albertine."

"Who shall I say is calling?"

"I work for Mr. Milieu — it's about Seward's death."

She let me in and led the way to a room where a young
woman sat at a table covered with papers. Financial
columns, train schedules, and a racing chart for the hippodrome.

The room was a mess. It was choked up with furniture,
no piece of which was in the right place.

Gort introduced me. Albertine got up, kicked a couple
of newspapers out of the way, and came to take my hand.

She was about five foot seven, a few inches shorter
than I am, with broad shoulders, full breasts, and round
hips. Her face revealed a girl of twenty-four, living hard.
Her plump cheeks showed lines near her mouth, her
"impudent expression" seemed less than fresh, and her
"laughing eyes" were bloodshot.

Her coarse brown hair needed a trim and the part was
crooked. She wore a dark housedress, almost a suit of
mourning, but without a jacket and scarf it seemed more
like a naughty negligee, especially when she moved and the
gap flashed a glimpse of cleavage.

This was *the* Albertine.

"You must be the new man," she said while she moved

a polo cap and a golf club off a chair to make room for me.

Her lips hardly moved when she talked. Her voice had a drawling, nasal sound.

"Don't go away, Gort," she said.

Gort came back. We all sat around the table.

"I hear you were seeing Seward."

"We weren't going steady, or anything like that," said Albertine. "We were just friends."

"He was working on the doomsday book," I said. "He was poking around, so I guess you were helping him."

"Maybe I could help you, too, if you've got enough money."

"I'll bet that's the pitch you made when you called Seward at the Californie."

"You think that was me?"

"It's going around town," I said. "You and Seward, behind Octave's back. Seward withdraws all that cash and winds up dead. I heard one gendarme say they were interested in talking with Albertine."

"They know where I live," she said.

"So he brought you the money and then left?" I said.

"Yeah."

"He just dropped it off?"

"Something like that."

"Then Octave gave him a ride?"

She raised her arms and stretched her back so that her breasts nearly fell out of her dress.

"I'd like to help you, but what's in it for me?" she said.

"Safety," I said.

"Non," she said.

I stood up to leave.

"Ah, come on," she said. "Don't be such a piss-vinegar. Stay for a drink or two, let me talk sense to you."

I sat down. Gort went out of the room.

"You're in a tough spot," I said. "Too old to play Juliet anymore."

"That's right," she said. "So I'm collecting my pension wherever I can. Be my friend and contribute generously."

"What comes next?" I asked. "A new role?"

"Maybe," she said, sighing and looking away. "Or maybe I'll just leave. I mean, further advance is not possible here."

Gort came back with a six-pack of coke, a bottle of rum, and a bowl of chipped ice. She sat for one drink then left the room. Albertine and I continued drinking, with me trying to trick more information out of her, while she tried to squeeze money out of me.

The night wore on. As she drank her lips started to move more and her words became more British. We finished the bottle. Finally she broke.

"All right, piss-vinegar, I'll play. You think it's not going to cost you, but I'll get mine in the end. What do you think of that?"

I made sounds of agreement. The pancakes in my gut were a big help but I wasn't sure I could watch my mouth.

"'Sright," she said. "I'm so bloody pished I'll tell you anything. An-ee-thing. Go 'head."

She said it a few times before I asked, "Why did Evan give you the money?"

"For dirt," she said, slapping the table. "Red-hot, scandalous dirt. Enough to blow this burg up, maybe even bring in the U.N. troops."

"Dirt on Octave?"

"Sure. Octave, Neuman, and even your boss."

"So that's why Neuman's after you, even though Octave was the one who killed Seward."

"Octave didn't kill Evan, get it?" She leaned close, breathing on my face while her eyes tried to focus. "He was already shot when we found him. Octave took him in his car to the doctor."

"So who shot him?"

"I don't know."

"Did you shoot him?"

"Naw," she said. "Why should I? It don't make no sense."

"You going to leave town, now that you got your big payoff?"

"Maybe, maybe non," she said. "I could always use more money."

•

It must have been past one o'clock when I left her sleeping on the table. Now that I really was drunk it seemed like I should see the tireman but he wasn't around as I sailed up the street. I pounded on the flophouse door for a long time before filly Albertine let me in. She gave me hell but it probably would've been worse if she knew where I'd been.

Somehow or another I got up to my room and caught what sleep I could.

I was roused out of bed by the police.

"That was a good idea you had the other day, about shutting down the Californie," said chief Neuman with relish. "We're going to do it now and thought you'd like to come along."

Apparently there was no time for a shave or a change of clothes. We piled into a police car and headed out of town with an entourage of several other squad cars and a flat bed truck. Everyone had a rifle or a riot gun, and pockets bulged with packages of ammunition.

"Good news," said Neuman. "That Webley you brought in turns out to be the murder weapon. Good job."

After a bone-jarring ride we arrived. The place looked different in the daylight, and it was surrounded by gendarmes. Two gendarmes were on the flatbed truck, taking off the tarp covering some machine — it turned out to be a Maxim gun, period-style machine gun.

"You can see this will be like shooting fish in a barrel," said Neuman, twirling his mustache. "I feel kind of bad, not giving Octave a chance. Hell, this is Europe — he'll only get a couple-three years in jail for killing Seward in jealous rage. He's not a bad homie, but there's no point in me trying to talk to him. He never did like me."

He looked at me. I kept quiet.

"Would you give it a try?" he asked.

"Yeah, I'll try."

"That's great," he said, a big smile busting out. "I really appreciate it. You talk sense to him, see if you can get him to come along without any trouble. You know, fish in a barrel, all that stuff."

"Yeah," I said and walked out toward the front door, making sure to keep my hands swinging empty at my sides.

I got to the door and knocked lightly on the glass. There was no sound from inside, so I knocked harder and rattled the knob.

"Clear out while you still can," said a voice from behind the door.

"I want to talk to Octave," I said.

"Go back to the fatass who sent you."

"I've got nothing to do with Neuman," I said. "I'm alone. Can Octave hear me?"

There was a pause. The voice said, "Yeah."

"I'm the guy who told Albertine that Neuman was framing you," I said. "I want five minutes to talk with you. I'll drop my gun out here if you say so. Let me in."

I waited there, between a rock and a hard place. Neuman couldn't be trusted. Octave was an unknown — it all depended on whether Albertine had talked to him about our chat. It felt like a long wait.

"We open, and you come in quick," said the voice. "No funny stuff."

"All right."

The lock clicked. I moved in as the door opened.

Guns behind me went off. A blizzard of glass erupted from the door and windows.

I dove down, twisting to face the open door. The trim

Browning No. 1 was in my hand and I flicked off the safety. I saw a gendarme with a rifle aimed at me, then the wood floor splintered a few inches from my face. I lined him up and squeezed the trigger twice. His mouth was moving like he was swearing as he fell to his knees.

Someone dragged me back by my feet. The door slammed shut.

I was out of the pan and in the fire.

"I wasn't in on that plan," I shouted above the racket.

"I dunno," said one voice. "Did he shoot high?"

"Nah," laughed another voice. "I saw him plug Pierre."

The shooting slowed, then stopped. The blinds were speckled with holes now. A dapper voice spoke in the darkness: "Marc, you and Sherm keep a lookout up here. The rest of us will go downstairs."

We went through the kitchen and down into a cellar that was like Ali Baba's cavern, filled to the ceiling with smuggled goods. There was a couch, a card table with some folding chairs, and another door.

There were four of them with me. Octave was handsome, almost pretty — that kind of sharp-dressing playboy that women go gaga over. Two of the others were the same type, but not outshining the boss in clothes or looks. The fourth was a plain guy who looked like a turtle — so out of place among these racetrack sheiks that I pegged him for the number two.

Octave drew a fat roll of cash from his pocket and gave it to the turtle-man, who then disappeared through the other door. Octave lit a cigarette, sat down at the table, and gestured for me to sit across from him. I sat.

"How long is Neuman going to play cowboys before he goes home?" he asked, his suave voice showing a hint of annoyance.

"He's after you this time," I said. "I think he's going all the way."

"All this for your predecessor?" he said with a contemptuous smile. "He knows enough law to know he's got nothing on me."

"He's not going to make you face a judge," I said. "He's not even going to arrest you."

"Non?"

"You're going to be killed resisting arrest, or something like that."

Octave gave a derisive snort. "What's his beef with you?"

"I guess I'm just a hair in the soup."

"Albertine said you were okay, for a miser."

"She's a charming dame," I said. "Will you tell me about Seward's murder?"

"What a cock up that was."

"Did you do it?"

"Non."

"Who did it?"

"I don't know."

"But you were there."

"That's the bitch of it," he said. "It starts to look like a fix for a frame-up. See, I got this call from a homie that night. I don't know who he was. He said that Seward was going to Albertine with a load of cash, then he hung up. Like it would mean something to me, like I'd care."

"You weren't jealous?"

"Non. But it was strange, a mystery, and I was curious. So I went over, and Gort turned me away at the door, so he was already there. What the hell, I was there so I —"

Octave was interrupted by the unmuffled sound of gunfire when the upstairs door was briefly opened. Marc and Sherm came down, looking a little shook up.

"I thought I'd stay and watch," said Octave, finishing his sentence. "I sat there in my coupé for a couple of minutes. When Seward came out he pretended he didn't see my car and started walking down the street. I thought I'd surprise him, give him a ride and tell him someone was spying on him. When I started the car, that's when the shots were fired, and Seward fell. I ran over to him, and he was messed up but still alert.

"Now I was in it deep. Albertine came out as I was dragging him back to the coupé. There's a doctor I know on the promenade, so I drove like hell but he died on us. We left him by the bandstand."

"Who would set you up like that?"

"I don't know," Octave said. "Seems like too much thinking for Neuman, but the way he's jumping on it, maybe he's the one."

"Now the trick is getting out of here alive," I said.

Octave snorted at that. Turtle man came back and held the door open, showing it fronted a tunnel. We all trooped down that shaft for fifty yards or more, then climbed up a ladder in a dry well to emerge in a copse of trees. A uniformed gendarme held open the door of a black car, saying "Hurry up, please."

I got in but my companions lingered, looking at the scene. The restaurant was getting shot up, the Maxim gun's ta-ta-ta-ta-ta roaring over the sounds of rifles and shotguns.

By the time Octave got in the car, the gendarme holding the door was dancing like he had to pee. Turtle took the wheel and we tore out of there.

"Let me off near the Grand Hotel," I said.

Turtle looked at Octave, who nodded. They dropped me off in front of the hotel and drove the police car away.

The doorman tried to stop me from entering since I was a mess: rumpled clothes I'd slept in, stubble on my hung-over face, and smelling of gunplay. I told him I had to report to Mr. Milieu and got past.

On my way to the stairs I saw the elevator with both new and old Liftboy in it, so I changed my plan and went halfway into the cage, blocking the closure of the door.

"Whoa," said the old Liftboy. "Wild night?"

"Yeah," I said. "I finally met that Albertine you keep telling me about."

"Yeah?"

"We had a good time, but now the Californie is all shot up to hell."

"It is?"

"Just tell me why you killed Seward," I said. Manager Malaprop was moving towards us, while the lobby-fixture "Man with Feather in Hat" was crossing behind him.

"But I didn't!"

"So that's the way it's going to be?" I said. "We can't stand here and argue —"

"Is there a problem?" said Manager, his hands fluttering around.

"Yeah," I said to him. "We need a private place for talking. He probably won't confess until I've worked him and I don't want everybody in the lobby to hear me yelling."

"Confess?" Manager adjusted the pince-nez glasses on his nose.

"That's right. Didn't you know he killed Evan Seward?"

Puzzled, Manager looked to the blushing Lift who had a quivering grin. Alarmed, Manager cleared his throat and said, "It is a spavine morning. Spavine weather we've been having."

"Isn't there a private room where we can talk? Staff room?"

"Yes, yes," said Manager. "This way." Before we moved away he turned to the new Liftboy and said, in an undertone, "You're on your own."

We followed his floating coattails to the office behind the lobby counter. I sat Lift down in one chair and myself in another. Manager hovered around.

"You love Albertine but you lost her from lack of money," I said. "You were at the Californie when Seward got the call, so then you called Octave, trying to set him up."

The boy looked cool as a cucumber and said nothing. I had to shake him up, so I started in on him.

"You were gaga over the dame. You were way out of your league — *mon dieu*, she's a major, and what are you? To buy her love you took on a second job with —"

"Non — please don't," he said. His face was so flushed it looked sunburned.

"You talked too much, boy. You were pushing me in the direction you wanted. I don't know why you didn't just leave town."

"Where would I go while she is still here?" he said. "I didn't mean to kill him."

I nodded, projecting all the sympathy I could fake.

"I didn't mean to," he said again. "I thought Octave would, but he didn't. Seward was just walking away. I knew then that I was the only one to feel jealous, and that was because I was the only one who really loved her."

Manager caught his breath at that. His eyes were brimming as if he were deeply moved by the story.

"I don't remember shooting," Lift said to Manager. "It was like the sound of the last shot woke me up from sleepwalking. I ran between the buildings into a dead-end, but Octave didn't chase me, he drove off with Seward. I figured he would take him to Doctor Steinman, so I walked over there. I was hoping that Seward would be all right."

"But he wasn't," I said.

"Non," said Lift. "He was there by the bandstand. Dead."

"Did you search him?"

"Non. I couldn't touch him."

"So that's why you sent the other Albertine, the filly."

"I just kept thinking that maybe he had some money on him, or maybe something valuable that she had given him."

"So you called the filly."

"Yeah."

"What did she find?"

"I don't know."

"Where's the gun?"

"I put it back under the counter at the Californie. Then I called the filly."

•

I walked him over to the police station. The gendarmes were pretty sore about how I had shot their Pierre, who was now in the hospital. Neuman talked about how he had a stern way of dealing with hostage takers, which is why they poured on the firepower after I had been "taken hostage" and the gangsters had refused to cooperate. They all forgot about it the moment I handed over the killer.

After that I went back to the Grand Hotel to freshen up and make my report to Mr. Milieu. From his cluttered bed he asked me all sorts of detailed questions, blowing his nose every few minutes. At one point he asked for my pistol and sniffed at it. When the story was finally told, he sighed and said:

"There is the sordid Balbec of reality here, all around us, and the Balbec of dream which is struggling to be born."

That sounded true enough, but I thought it would be a very messy birth.

JUNKBOY AND DEBUTANTE

Matt Hernando, a lanky young low-towner with a blonde Mohawk, leaned against his motorcycle at the Mojave Spaceport fence, waiting for the night launch of the *Rhyolite Express*. His muscles ached from hours of cutting up metal, separating salvage from junk in the rocket graveyard where he worked after school. But he never tired of watching the cargo rockets lift off and land at the spaceport.

He thought he was alone at the observation area until he heard the click of high heels approaching. He turned to see a debutante in red walking toward him across the dark empty parking lot.

He shook his head and looked again. High-Town for sure, and Matt ran his hand across his hair until his fingers touched the metal at the back.

"Hey," she called softly, as if they were old friends.

"Uh, he-llo," he said, stuttering in awkward High-Town.

She stepped close enough to see the long scars on his face and the low-town haircut. She faltered for a second, glancing back over her shoulder, but then she regained her poise and walked up to him.

"Can you help me, please?" she asked, looking up into his face.

Her red dress left her pale shoulders bare, and long black gloves came up past her elbows. There was a dark band around her neck, and her shoulder-length black hair had a big red bow on the right side. She was a deb fresh from some robocratic function, in an unlikely place.

His cyber-heart thumped raggedly, so he set it to Steady before he answered.

"Sure," he said. "Your car —?"

"I need to get out to the *Rhyolite Express*," she said.

"Too late," he said. He checked his beat up old wristwatch. "It's going any —"

Launch pad 5 lit up with a fiery roar and the rocket leaped into the sky on a pillar of exhaust.

The girl gasped, her hand flying to her throat. By the rocket's glare Matt saw her blue eyes before his gaze was drawn to the necklace. If it was real, it was wealth beyond Matt's wildest dreams, tempting him with instant criminal impulses. It glittered like a starry band, like the Milky Way above the smooth white slopes of her breasts. He saw she was cold.

Which do you want? he asked himself. *The girl or the necklace?*

"When will it be back?" she asked, looking up at him with big eyes.

He decided.

"Around dawn, usually," he said, taking off his motorcycle jacket. He draped the jacket around her shoulders, careful not to touch her with his hands. He resisted the urge to tuck in his dirty white T-shirt.

"Thanks," she said, blinking back tears. "Can you take me home, to Babel Nouveau? I'll pay you."

"You don't got a car?"

"No."

"How did you get here?"

She sighed. "It's a long story."

"Why don't I just take you over to the spaceport where you can get a taxi?"

"No, no!" she said. "I can't — please, just take me home."

"Okay," he said, sensing a possible trap — she might be the honey bait for either a criminal act or a robot police entrapment. But he swung onto the saddle and kick-started the engine to life.

"Put your arms in the jacket," he said as he put his riding goggles in place. "Come sit behind me. Closer. You got to, uh, hug me, around the waist. Put your fingers between your fingers — weave them together. I'm your shield. Okay, here we go."

God Almighty, he thought as they started forward. *This is every guy's dream come true.*

As they left the parking lot they passed a robot police car coming in. The car made a sudden U-turn and came after them with lights and siren blazing.

Matt hesitated.

"No!" she screamed. "Go! Go!"

They blasted away at full throttle. Matt rode hard and fast, weaving among the many cars on R14. Reaching the left lane he cut across the meridian, kicking up a spray of sand, and headed south, opposite the way they wanted to go. The police car followed. He continued weaving, wondering what sort of deb would run from the police.

A fake one, he thought. *A hooker or a thief — maybe a jewel thief?*

He took the Rocket Town exit, blazing through a maze of backstreets and narrow alleys, and doubled back, losing the cops. On the highway heading north, he reduced speed and hid behind trucks. He saw the new robot police luftcycle followed by three more robot police cars, all zooming south to support a sweep of Rocket Town. The last one was Comandante Martinek's car, and Matt grinned. One over on the metal bastard.

Matt took the sweeping left curve onto R58, heading

west towards Bakersfield. Babel Nouveau, home to a half million robots and humans, towered over three thousand feet into the sky, looking like a stack of three gigantic hubcaps on a squat base. Surrounding it was a wide greenbelt of chaparral forest and meadows, enclosed in turn by a ring of country villas set on artificial hills, the ramparts of High-Town.

The debutante directed him into this periphery, to a section called Blue Villas. Matt noticed that instead of house numbers there were unique signs and symbols hanging at each gate — a flower at one, a clock face with hands at twelve at another, a weird bottle at a third. She had him stop at a dwelling with a carved sign of a duck that showed a dull greenish blue when illuminated by his headlight. Matt could see a hexagonal teahouse to the left and the main house to the right, perched atop a mound beyond the concrete wall. They had the high gabled construction denoting wealth and prestige.

He killed the engine. She got off the bike stiffly and stretched her legs.

"Whew," she said softly. "Thank you so much. I'll just go inside and get the money."

"Sure," he said, shrugging. He figured she might not come back out at all, and wondered if he was about to lose his jacket, but she took only a few steps before she stopped cold.

"What's the matter?" he whispered.

"Something's wrong," she said. "It's too dark."

"Maybe your folks went out," he said.

"No," she said, coming back to his side. "Something has happened." Her voice trembled and her face was pinched with fear. "I'm scared."

"You're kidding me!" He peered up at the dark villa. It looked ordinary enough.

"They would've left lights on," she said in a rush. "They'd be worried about me." She started to cry. "Please, please help me."

"All right, all right," he said, trying to come up with a plan. He couldn't take her home to his mom, he couldn't take her to the police . . . "I know somewhere. Let's go."

He headed onto R58 heading back toward the spaceport, trying to figure out her angle as they rode along.

Is she good or bad? he wondered. *If she's bad, she just blew it — she could've gone off into the house and left me.*

In the last hills before Mojave he took the off ramp and rode up to Inspiration Point.

Since it was a Tuesday night in winter, nobody else was at the parking lot overlooking the desert valley. Matt slowed to a stop at the end of the lot where a dirt road started. When he cut the engine they could hear the whir of the wind turbines in the hills behind them.

"Why are we stopping here?" she asked, not moving to dismount.

"Stretch our legs," he said with some irony, testing her. "We got a couple miles of dirt road ahead."

"Oh, okay." She hopped off and dutifully flexed her long legs.

Matt shook his head as he dismounted, wondering if she was faking naiveté.

"What's your name, anyway?"

"Erica, Erica Delagroux." She held out her hand. "And you would be . . . ?"

He wiped his hand on his jeans before he took up her hand, his doubts momentarily swept aside.

"Matt Hernando," he mumbled. "Call me Matt."

"All right, Matt." She turned to look at the view, taking in the spaceport and the bright central city, Rocket Town glowing like embers, and R14 a march of streetlights. "It's beautiful."

"Come here often?" he said with a smirk, watching her reaction closely.

"No, never," she said. She gave him a look of wary appraisal. "It must be popular, then? Among those who cannot afford a love hotel?"

Matt felt his face grow hot and went on the offensive. "I was wondering about that necklace."

"And I was wondering about the metal plate on the back of your head," she shot back.

"I don't want to talk about that."

"I don't want to talk about the necklace."

They glared at each other until Matt broke his gaze to watch a rocket landing at the spaceport.

"That's the *Beatty Bullfrog*," he said. "God, I wish I could go up on a rocket like that."

"You want to go to space?" she asked.

"Yeah. There must be work for a junkman up there. Earth Orbit, on the Moon, or even Mars."

"I'm terrified of it," she said. "I'll have to go in a few years — the nuptial flight — and I'd trade with you, if I could. But I can't."

Matt felt giddy, as if she had just kissed him. He adjusted his heart to Steady, but it didn't change anything — a bug to report to Sandy.

"What are you doing?" she asked.

"Nothing," he said. "So what's your dream, huh? Marry wealth, and go up from there?"

"No, I just want to have fun," she said. "Everything is so artificial at Babel Nouveau, I want to see real nature and real people. I want to simplify my life. Maybe have a quiet little farm."

"Huh," said Matt. "So I want to go up, and you want to go down."

"I guess so."

"Well come on, let's go."

They rode up the dirt road into wind turbine country. The road branched among the towering windmills, and branched a few more times until they suddenly came upon an old farmhouse.

Matt left her by the bike, going up on the dark porch to knock on the door. He heard the 3V inside go quiet, so he knocked again. After a few moments the porch lights came

MICHAEL ANDRE-DRIUSSI

on and an old woman opened the door.

"Sorry Granny —"

"Matt, you're in trouble," she said.

"Yeah," he said. "Well, no, it's not me, it's her."

"A girl?" She squinted to peer out. "Matt!"

"No, it's not like that — let me talk to you, inside."

Once the door was closed he told her the whole story.

"Wow," said Granny.

"The thing's fishy to me," he said. "Why's a deb scared of the police? I think she might be a fake who stole the necklace or something."

"What about that duck house?"

"I don't know," he said, looking at the floor. "I mean, I didn't see anything wrong there. Maybe she knew a villa that was empty."

"Maybe so, maybe so," said Granny. "But then it sounds like she was planning on getting you to pick her up."

"She could be just winging it. But anyway, can she stay here? She seems scared, like, for real."

"Well, a day's okay," said Granny. "You only need a day 'til the next launch, right? I don't want trouble with the robots — this would be a lot of squeeze."

The robot police out-ranked local police, they could go anywhere, but they focused on strategic sites like the transportation hub of spaceport/Rocket Town, and energy producers like Granny's windfarm.

"Great, thanks!" said Matt, producing a calculated boyish grin. "I'll look around in the morning, try to figure things out. And hey, she's got fantasies about farm life, so maybe you can get some work out of her."

Matt called the deb and introduced her to his grandmother, then rode home to the modest house in Low Town. His widowed mother was asleep in front of the 3V, but woke up when he turned off the set. He apologized, and went off to bed.

He dialed down his heart and fell asleep before his

head hit the pillow, but his sleep was not so mechanical. In his dreams he relived the moment at the make-out place, only it was better because she sat on the ground, cradling his head in her lap as they watched the night sky with its glittering stars, unblinking planets, and fiery rockets. She leaned down and kissed him upside down. She was his girl-friend. They rode on his motorcycle in the daytime for everyone to see, his heart swelling with pride.

The next morning he took the train to high school, resisting the urge to check up at Granny's. His best friend Roy was waiting for him at the gate in his usual black sun-glasses, his long hair, bleached bone white, fanned out on his black leather jacket.

Matt quietly told him about the previous night's adven-ture, ending with, "So did you hear about anything hap-pening last night?"

"There was a debutante event over at the spaceport," said Roy. "Not that I follow that stuff, you know, but I didn't hear about any trouble."

"No stolen necklace?"

"Nope. But I didn't look at the news, either, so I don't know."

"I was going to check this morning," said Matt, "but if my mom saw, she'd get suspicious."

"Let's just use the library right now."

They looked at local news on a school library terminal and found nothing relevant.

"You busy after school?" asked Matt.

"Nah."

"Great. I need your help."

"You got it."

After school let out, Matt got his motorcycle and rode over to their hangout, the Fino diner. Roy was already there, sitting on his own motorcycle.

"I didn't hear anything all day," said Roy. "Did you?"

"No."

"Well, you want to snoop around over at B.N.?" He

said the nickname for Babel Nouveau like they all did — *bien*.

"Let's eat first," said Matt.

•

It was still light out as Matt led the way into the Blue Villa district, and when they passed the one with the duck sign he took in the B.N. police cars, the crime scene van, and the police tape. He tried not to stare.

That's when he noticed the shiny red hovercar parked nearby. Everybody knew that was Baklanov's sports-huv, and Matt saw the blond gangster sitting inside, talking to one of his associates as though the crime scene were a 3V show. Matt rode on by, but felt their eyes burning his back.

He turned the whole thing over in his head, looking for a way to test something, anything. The *Rhyolite Express* should have landed at around dawn.

Where in the spaceport would the pilot be now? he thought. *The concourse, the hotel, one of the bars. Tomorrow's launch is at 05:30, so he'll go to bed early. No bars now because of pre-flight rules. Try the hotel.*

From the phone booth in a Mom & Pop store he made a call to the spaceport hotel and asked to speak to the pilot of the *Rhyolite Express*. The room phone rang twice.

"Hello?" said a gruff voice. In the background was the sound of a 3V show. Matt was so surprised at having made contact he nearly hung up the phone.

"Hello?" said the man again.

"Is this the pilot of the *Rhyolite Express?*" asked Matt.

"Yeah. Who's this?"

"Who went up last night?"

"So?"

"There's this deb," said Matt, lamely. "Last night."

He expected a sarcastic comment, but instead there was quiet for a beat. The 3V show went silent. Finally the man spoke.

"Is she okay? She wasn't at . . . the place."

"Yeah, she's okay. Can —"

"Let me talk to her," said the pilot.

"She's not with me right now."

"Where is she, then?"

"She's at a safe place."

"What's your name?"

"Matt Hernando."

"How do I know you're telling the truth, Matt?"

"I don't know," said Matt. "Look, can she try again? I mean, what would be a good time to try?"

The pilot was quiet for a moment.

"Around four a.m.," he said. "She knows the place."

"Okay, bye," said Matt. He hung up.

•

When night came Matt and Roy went out to Granny's windfarm.

"Hello Roy," said Granny with strained nonchalance. "I haven't seen you since apple picking time."

"Where is she?" asked Matt.

"In the back," said Granny. "You find out what's going on?"

"Nothing in the news —"

"But the beanpoles are over at the villa," said Roy, giving her a significant look.

"Too hot for me," said Granny. "Take her to the police — the humans. Let them sort it out."

"What if she don't want to go?"

"I don't know," said Granny with a sigh.

"She give you any trouble?"

"What do you mean?"

"Did she, like, use the phone, or try to walk away?"

"No, no, nothing like that," said Granny. "Now listen to me. She's the real thing, all right? Way out of your league. You get it?"

115

"Yeah, yeah."

"I don't want to get busted for kidnapping, or you, either. You hear me? If she's gone off on a joy ride, we're the ones who are going to get in trouble, not her. Her kind don't get in trouble."

"Yeah, all right."

"All right then," she said, smoothing her farm dress. "I said my piece. Wait here and I'll go get her."

Matt and Roy shared a look then looked away, fidgeting while the hum of the wind turbines grew louder in the quiet.

Granny came back with a farm girl in blue jeans and a yellow shirt. It took Matt a few seconds to recognize this plain Jane as the dazzling Erica. Her big hair was now simple and modest, her face had no trace of make-up, and her high heels had been replaced with a pair of worn sneakers.

"Wow," said Matt. "Roy, this is, uh, Erica. Erica, Roy."

"Hey," said Erica, not offering her hand. It made her seem just like a Low Towner. She glanced at Granny, who nodded her approval.

"I guess we'd better head out," said Matt.

Erica put on an old coat and a rucksack. "Thanks for letting me stay," she said. "And for the clothes."

"It's nothing," said Granny. "Just drop 'em off next time you're in the neighborhood."

Before Matt started his engine he asked Erica, "You got the necklace?"

"In the coat pocket. Inside pocket."

"Good."

"Where are we going, anyway?"

"Low Town. Roy knows a place."

They rode down past Inspiration Point and took R58 west to Low Town, that grimy but functional landscape completely alien to Erica. They rode past a series of strip malls separated by the dirty industries of recycling centers and repair bays, punctuated here and there with coffee shops, pawnbrokers, Mom & Pop corner markets, and tattoo parlors.

They entered the warehouse district and pulled into the back area of a warehouse.

"Here we are," said Roy. "Nice and quiet."

"You still want to get on that rocket, right?" said Matt to Erica.

"Ye-ee-ah," she said, signaling some unspoken qualifiers.

"Okay," said Matt. "That means we've got a lot of time to kill. The plan is to keep someone guarding you at all times. I'll watch first, then Roy, then me again, like that. But first I got to go pick up some stuff, okay? I'll be right back."

Matt went to a corner market to buy supplies. As he was paying there was a news bulletin on the 3V, a brief item that ended with a picture of Deb Erica Delagroux in her red dress.

Matt went back to the hideout and settled in for his shift. As Roy rode off, Erica asked him, "What's wrong?"

"What do you mean?"

"I mean, you look like something happened."

"Your folks are dead," he said. "It was on the 3V just now." He held her up as she started to fold. "The robot police are looking for you, they put your picture up. Listen, maybe I should just take you to the human police and clear this up?"

"No!" she cried, pounding his chest. "No, no, no! I can't trust them."

"What?"

"They might have killed my parents."

"That's crazy!"

"No, it isn't," she said, knuckling away tears. "My father was an undercover agent for the orbital government. I only found out last night. He had proof of robot police corruption, and ties to organized crime!"

"Welcome to the real world, High Town," said Matt.

"A night in Rocket Town would prove that to anybody, no matter how stupid. The robots squeeze, but they don't kill . . . I don't think."

She started crying again, so Matt shook her. "Go on. What happened last night?"

"He — he put the necklace on me and said it belongs to the pilot of the *Rhyolite Express*. He told me to slip away from the ball and meet the pilot on the concourse — I would say 'Diamonds are a girl's best friend' and he would say 'A silver mine is just a digger looking for a heart of gold.' Then I'd give him the necklace and leave."

"Wait," said Matt. "You weren't going up, just handing over the stuff?"

"Yes, but I couldn't get there in time. I tried to get to the concourse, but robot police were blocking all the ways. When I went back to the ball, the police were already there, questioning people."

"Whoa."

"Yeah, so I left. I couldn't go through the concourse, so I went outside and started walking around the fence. That's when I saw you."

She looked over her shoulder and said, "I'm worried about having the necklace in Low Town." She clutched at his jacket. "Here, you take it."

"*Me?* But, but why?"

"I trust you."

His cyber heart skipped a beat.

"Okay," he said, accepting the necklace with numb fingers.

He told her the plan, how he had phoned the pilot and arranged for them to meet on the concourse before four. They talked a bit longer and then she slept on the pavement next to the wall, resting her head on her folded arm. He sat there, watching over her, his motorcycle nearby, and after a while he took the necklace out to look at again, to see that it really existed.

It twinkled in his hands like stars. He could take it to

Mojave right now, buy his way onboard the *Garlock Gazelle* and be in orbit before she woke up.

But she had said she trusted him.

•

Roy showed up at eleven, walking his bike in from the street so he wouldn't wake Erica. They conferred in whispers. Roy told him that the diner was abuzz over the murder mystery, and was interrupted by the noise of a hovercar going by on the empty street.

Matt wheeled his bike out to the street and started it up. The hovercar came back, Baklanov's sports-huv, the gangster and his flashy passengers talking to each other with easy animation, as if they were just cutting through the warehouse district from one party to another. Matt felt his heart jump. He dialed it down to Steady to avoid drawing attention to himself, and then rode off in the other direction.

He went home, lied to his mother, and went to sleep. After a few hours his internal clock woke him up, and then he sneaked out of the house.

When he returned to the hideout he found Roy's bike on its side, with Roy curled up on the ground. Erica was gone.

"Roy!" said Matt. He dropped his bike and rushed over. "What happened? Where's Erica?"

He rolled Roy over and saw his face was swollen with bruises.

"They got her," said Roy with a muffled croak.

"Who got her?"

"Baklanov," said Roy.

"I should've known — I saw him but I tried to play it cool. Damn!"

Roy coughed and said, "They want the necklace." His speech was slurred.

"The necklace!" said Matt, feeling a sudden chill go up

his spine as reality threatened to shift on him again. "How'd they know about the necklace?"

"I dunno."

"They beat you pretty bad," said Matt. "They hurt her?"

"No, they gave her a shot of some dope to make her talk. Gave me one, too. She told them you have the necklace. I told them where you live — I'm sorry, but I couldn't stop!"

"It's okay," said Matt, fear and anger rising in him. "I should've been here."

"He followed me from the diner," said Roy. "My fault."

"You talked about Erica at the diner?"

"Hell no. They were looking for your yellow Mohawk. Someone at the diner told 'em we were tight. They followed me. I didn't notice."

"Where's he now?"

"At the Arena. He says he will trade Erica for the necklace, but they will kill her at three o'clock."

"He's bluffing," said Matt.

"I dunno," said Roy. "He made it sound like they killed her folks."

Matt tried to calm his thoughts, his mind awhirl with all the sudden changes. Considering his options, he could take the necklace to the Arena, or he could take the necklace to the spaceport. Erica would want him to take it to the spaceport, but the thought of putting her in danger like that made him feel sick. He wasn't certain that Baklanov would make a fair trade, anyway — he might even kill them both. So Matt was supposed to just go in there by himself with odds like that?

"Can you ride?" he asked.

"I don't think so," said Roy. "My head's messed up from the drug. I think they screwed up my bike, too."

Matt checked the motorcycle, painfully aware that he was running out of time as the options were dwindling.

"We'll fix it later," he said. "Right now I got to go over to the Arena."

"Good luck," said Roy.

Matt started his motorcycle and rode out onto the street. He turned up his cyber heart a notch to help him think.

The hangout called the Arena was an abandoned motel courtyard on the other side of town, in the bad section known as the Pits. As Matt rode along he came upon a couple of human police cars and realized with a guilty start that he was speeding. He slowed down with the icy fear that Erica would be killed if he was delayed by the police giving him a ticket.

But that gave him a different idea.

He sped up alongside the leading patrol car, where he hit the hood with his fist and sped away.

The car lit up and gave chase.

Matt rode like a demon, bobbing and weaving in the light traffic, going through red lights accompanied by the sound of screeching tires, blaring horns, and bending fenders.

When he had four cops on his tail he thought it might be enough, but by the time he got to the Arena he had six.

He rode into a menacing scene where Erica was tied up to a pole and the three gangsters had their pistols out. They pointed them at Erica, but when they saw how Matt was barreling toward them they shifted to aim at him.

Then the cops arrived and all hell broke loose.

Matt threw his bike into a slide heading right at Baklanov, like a bowling ball going for the kingpin. The gangster jumped out of the way and kept moving off. Matt stood up in the dust cloud and cut Erica's bonds with his jack knife. The police were yelling and the sports-huv started up with a roar.

Matt pulled Erica over to the bike, and she got on behind him. They faced a wall of headlights through the settling dust. Matt gunned the engine and drove toward them, then veered off to the narrow side entrance.

And then they were free, the police busy with Baklanov and his boys. Erica clung to him, her forehead hot on his neck, and the emotional surge that went through him was so much like his dream that he felt like yelling out loud. He turned his heart down to Steady but it didn't seem to work — another bug report for Sandy.

•

Go where it's least expected, Matt decided. He rode calmly and quietly toward Babel Nouveau, passing the villas, crossing the chaparral, until they were at a robotics lab literally in the shadow of the beetling arcology. The complex was dark, closed for the night, but at the back was a small separate building off in the corner where a lone window glowed.

Matt parked the bike and turned it off. An old man's face appeared in a window. "Who's out there?" He wore big glasses and his unruly white hair was backlit so that it looked like a spiky halo.

"It's me, Matt!"

"Trouble with your parts?"

"We just got some questions."

"'We'? Who's that with you?"

"This is . . . Erica."

"A girl? On a late night date and you come here?"

The old man climbed down from a chair and disappeared from the window.

Matt turned to Erica. "He don't watch the news."

A moment later the door opened.

"Come in, come in," said the elderly man in his white lab coat. "Give the old night owl some company."

"Erica, this is Doctor Lomeli."

Erica, forgetting her low-town persona, stepped forward and took the scientist's hand.

"It is a pleasure to meet you, doctor," she said, all silk

and honey.

"Call me Sandy," he said, beaming. "Everybody does. Here, let's go inside."

Robotic torsos and heads cluttered the workbenches, the counters, and on the floor. Computer boards and servo parts were stacked in the gaps between loose arms and legs. They followed him to a roll top desk at the back where a bright lamp cast the room's light.

"Matt, you're looking a bit dusty!" said Sandy. "You were dirt racing and you did a power-slide, right?"

"Yeah."

"You just had to impress her."

"Yeah."

Sandy smiled. "I don't blame you. But still, be careful! Now go clean up in the washroom."

"But —"

"Matt, this is a laboratory! I'll talk with your friend here."

"All right."

Sandy began chattering as Matt turned away.

"I'm so happy to meet a new friend of Matt's. He doesn't seem to have many friends. They see that metal plate in his head, but when they realize he doesn't have the usual cyborg arms or legs or what-have-you, they get confused and think he must have a robot brain!"

Even in the washroom Matt could hear him. It was embarrassing, and he was glad he wasn't in the same room.

"But the cybernetic stuff isn't in his head, it's in his body — his circulatory and adrenal systems. He can control his heart — well, usually he can, but now I wonder!"

Matt bit off a curse — What was the old fool saying?

"Still, there's a danger when he revs it up too high, he can give himself a heart attack. Literally! Even a boy, a young man like that! So please keep that in mind."

She said something Matt couldn't make out.

"Yes, it was experimental," said Sandy. "I couldn't see much use for it until the accident — it killed his father, you know, the accident did."

Matt's heart needed to Steady, but to adjust it seemed like a crutch for a cripple. He hurried to finish up instead.

"No, of course not," said Sandy. "He doesn't talk about it. They were riding off-road and they ran into some toxic waste illegally dumped. His father was something of a hero for the way he handled it. Sadly, he died of massive organ failure a few weeks later, but we were able to save Matt."

Matt stomped out, cleaned up, waving the necklace.

"We got to take this to the spaceport!" he said, thrusting it at Sandy. "But first I want to know what it is!"

"It's very pretty," said Sandy, taking it gingerly. After looking it under the light, he asked, "Is it stolen?"

"No," said Matt. "It was on loan."

"Hmm," said Sandy, telegraphing skepticism.

"Are those real gems, or is it fake?"

"I'm not a gemologist, but they sure look . . . now wait a second."

"What?" said Matt as Sandy swung a hands-free magnifier lamp over.

"I'll be damned," he said. "They look like data crystals. Here, let's see." Sandy rummaged around in the piles of equipment and pulled up a device with a wire probe. He touched the probe to a "gem" and looked at the readout on the device.

"Yes, it's a data crystal. What a strange thing."

"Does it have a message?"

"Well it *could* have a lot." Sandy fiddled with the device. "I can't tell — it's encrypted. Now what's this all about?"

Matt told him the short version.

". . . so that's why we got to get it to the rocket before five thirty."

"Assuming the robots are there, how are you going to get past security?"

"We'll miss the meeting with the pilot, so they might give up on the spaceport side," said Matt. "They'll think that window is shut, too close to launch time."

"If they think that, they would be right."

"We can go through the graveyard," said Matt with a confidence he only half-felt. "It's like what Erica was trying the first time, but I work there, so I have access codes. We'll ride up when the crew van is dropping him off at the rocket, before he climbs up. She will hand it over and then we'll blitz out of there before the cops come."

"It's too dangerous for her, with cops chasing you the whole way."

"I will stay," said Erica. "You can go faster without me."

"They'll be looking for two on a bike," said Sandy, nodding.

"But —"

"I can't go by myself — I can't ride a motorcycle," said Erica. "But I can ask you to do it, as a favor for me."

He looked down into her face. She looked up into his.

"You . . . sure?" he asked.

She nodded.

"I won't let you down," he said.

"I know."

•

R58 had plenty of traffic, mostly semi trucks, alone or in convoys, trying to get through the winter twilight before the morning rush began. Matt rode at the speed limit down the long straight slope from the highlands to the Mojave Desert. When he saw the sweeping, elevated curve to the right where it becomes the R14/R58 interchange, he knew he was only fifteen miles away.

Then he spotted the robot police luft-cycle parked on the side of the road. It was new to the Mojave area, unique. People called it "the Sandshark" or "Martinek's pet," or maybe that was the robot who rode it.

As he went past, the luft-cycle suddenly started up, rising to hover on a column of air. In his mirror he saw it pull into traffic. Matt set his heart to Steady, playing it cool.

The luft-cycle, right behind him, lit up with lights and siren, then rushed up on the left. Matt stayed cool, hoping it would pass by, but instead it moved to box him in and the robot's amplified voice said, "Motorcycle, pull over!"

Matt turned his heart up.

A passenger car in front of Matt boxed him in, with a semi-truck passing on the left. The car in the right lane was speeding to get out of the way. Matt amped his heart, gunned his bike and shot through the closing gap.

Roaring along in the right lane, Matt thought he had blocked the cop behind a row of cars, but as he drifted back into the center lane he was astonished to see the luft-cycle hop over the car. Only military hovercraft could make jumps like that.

As the cop closed in on him they entered the sweeping curve right. A semi-truck loomed in the center lane, with a passenger car on the left moving to pass it.

The racing instinct is to go to the inside of a curve, but Matt wanted to go left, and his jacked-up heart made him think he could pull it off.

Again Matt threaded the needle, cutting off the passenger car, his bike shuddered under the centripetal force. As he fought to keep control he kept an eye on the guardrail whizzing past and the fifty-foot drop beyond it.

In his mirror he saw the luft-cycle again hopping over a blocking passenger car. He glanced back and saw it drifting toward the guardrail, lacking the tire-to-road friction to match the centripetal force.

The luft-cycle smashed down onto the guardrail. For an instant it seemed as though it might bounce back onto the road, but instead it tipped over the edge and disappeared, its hover fans roaring in the void. A moment later Matt heard a muffled explosion.

The road straightened out into R14 and two police cars

were on his tail, followed by the comandante's car.

Dodging and weaving, Matt broke away from them, extending his lead. The spaceport was off to his left, the rocket field a few miles out, and the lane reflectors of R14 stretching out before him, looked like stars in the sky. He turned his heart down.

Matt slowed just enough on his way down the off ramp for Rocket Town, then sped through the red light, making a beeline for the rocket graveyard.

He skidded to a stop at the street gate and punched in his access code. The gate slowly began moving aside. Matt shot through and punched the close-gate button on the other side just as the police cars came screaming into view. He laughed in triumph and hightailed it into the junkyard's middle, a canyon-country of metallic buttes and spires.

There was only one way to the spaceport debris gate. Somehow Matt had to find a way to block that road to cars. He wished he could just push over one of the derelict rockets so it would lie across the road. He couldn't, of course, but it gave him an idea.

He sped up the road to a spot with a work platform holding a section of an old SRB side-rocket. He hopped off his bike and rushed up onto the platform where he kicked out the chocks holding the rocket steady on the side toward the road. On the other side of the rocket he put his shoulder to it and gave a hard push. It rolled off to land in the road, giving him great satisfaction as a car obstacle.

Back on his bike, he raced to the debris gate. He punched in his access code and muttered when the readout said "Access denied." He punched it in again, more carefully. When the readout repeated itself, his blood ran cold — the cops had communicated with the spaceport and they had locked the gate.

Matt took out the mini bolt cutter from his tool kit, and rode along the narrow path by the fence until he was out of sight of the debris gate. He turned off his bike and got to work, snipping a doorway large enough to ride through.

"Come out, Matt Hernando," said comandante Martinek through a bullhorn. "You're locked in."

Snip. Snip. Snip.

"We got the girl, Matt."

That made him pause. Snip. Snip.

"She's a fake — did you know that? She's a professional criminal."

It was a lie, but it felt half-true. Snip.

"Erica Delagroux died in the Blue Villa robbery. Bring out the necklace now and the robot judge will go easy on you. You were just a tool, a dupe."

Matt saw the crew van already heading back to the spaceport from pad 5 at the same moment he heard the metallic sound of the SRB being rolled away. He hurried, making the last few snips, then dropped the cutter and wheeled his bike through the hole. The police cars were already up at the debris gate, the robots beginning to fan out to search for him, when he kicked his motorcycle to life and took off across the miles-wide safety perimeter of the rocket field.

The pre-launch sirens were blaring as Matt raced across the launch field. Rockets towered at each of the six pads, waiting their turn. The *Rhyolite Express,* a trusty old DC-Y, was at pad 5, nearly six miles away.

On the open flat surface Matt looked back to see he was losing his lead. As he looked ahead again, ghostly streamers floated off the towering rockets, an incidental hallucination that served as a warning about his overworking heart. He turned it down, riding methodically but fast. His supreme self-confidence evaporated and cold fear began to rake him.

The *Rhyolite Express* grew steadily, its 130 feet of stark height seeming more pronounced without any buildings near it. It was like a four-sided tower on a desolate plain. Matt had to slow down but he still came in fast with a long slide that took him from the pavement across the blast pit grating, practically underneath one of the eight rocket nozzles.

The smell of water in the blast pit came to him as he hopped up. The rocket looked impossibly high from the base. A hatch opened up three-quarters of the way up that long wedge-shape, and a man leaned out to yell, "Up here, kid!"

The hatch was thirty yards up at the end of a rung ladder. Matt cranked his heart up to the limit and started climbing for his life.

He glanced down once, but it was too much.

Halfway up, he began thinking he was near Granny's windfarm, climbing a wind turbine on a dare. Over the pulsing swoosh of the turbine he heard the screech of cars coming to a hard stop behind him, far away. It didn't make sense, yet it filled him with fear.

"Come down off there!" commanded a bullhorn voice.

Comandante Martinek. Matt faltered for an instant, feeling dizzy, on the verge of hallucinating. He recovered, racing up.

Sounds popped behind him, starry shapes appeared on the metal surface around him in a constellation he could almost recognize. He faltered at a sharp pain in his left leg.

He climbed up more slowly, hindered by his hurt leg. The pilot appeared at the hatch and started firing back at the police.

"Come on, kid!"

Only three yards to go. Matt could hardly see the rungs for the stars.

Only two yards to go. The pilot stopped shooting and reached down. A new flurry of bullets drove him back inside.

"Climb up, climb up!"

A blow to Matt's lower back hurt like hell. He slipped a rung but caught himself. His legs were jelly.

One yard to go.

His vision grew dark at the edges. He willed himself

into a final surge and flopped halfway through the hatch. The pilot hauled him in and pulled the hatch closed.

"You did great, kid," he said as he manhandled Matt into the co-pilot's acceleration couch and belted him in. Matt didn't respond, concentrating on performing the heart-attack procedure he had only practiced before. He lay there inert, his lips shaping unspoken words. As he fought against death the unsuspecting pilot went through his pockets and found the necklace.

Matt came through it after the pilot moved away saying something about the orbital government. Drenched with sweat and gasping, he found himself staring up at the monitor showing an image of his motorcycle on the ground. As the pilot scrambled into his couch, Matt realized he was looking at the landing camera's view.

He saw the bright red fuel tank and the white lettering he knew spelled "Yamaha." It was a part of his life, almost a part of his body, now separated from him.

The pilot flipped a switch. The motorcycle was blackened for an instant by rocket fire before the blast tossed it away. The ground dropped away like a trapdoor opening.

Hang on, Erica, he prayed as the g forces bore down on him. *I'm coming right back to you. It'll only be eight hours. Sandy will keep you safe. I don't know what will happen next, but I'll be there for you, I swear. I'm your shield.*

DAUGHTER OF PLANT AND WOMAN

As the wife sat fanning herself by the window, a wondrous, delicious aroma came to her from the herb woman's garden below. It quickened her blood and gave her powerful cravings. She awakened her husband and pointed out the desired plants, which happened to be the newest hybrids in the garden.

"I want to eat a few of those," she told him.

"Wait until after nightfall," he said, and he went back to his Italian siesta.

When it was dark midnight, the husband crept over the wall, quickly stole a handful of the greens, and returned home. His wife ate the plunder and declared it delicious, but instead of quelling her appetite, the salad inflamed her desire to eat more.

So, the next night the husband again slipped over the wall and took two handfuls, thinking that this amount would satisfy his wife's cravings. Unfortunately it did not, and she became rapacious — she wanted more of those greens, and refused to eat anything else.

On the third night the husband again went over the wall, and this time he took four handfuls — all that remained. Just then the herb woman caught him.

131

"Who is this flying goat that is eating my fodder every night?" she said, and when she opened her lantern, she recognized him. He stood rapt, as if held by a net she had cast over him. "You! Rapscallion, why do you plunder my garden by night while others come to my front door by day?"

"These greens, good woman Gothel," he said. "I can find them in no other place, but my wife refuses to eat anything else." He told her the whole shameful story, and as he did so her anger faded, replaced by interest in the curious details.

Gothel had intended that the new simple would be used as a curative for horses — specifically she was hoping to aid her neighbor the stable master. But, the simple itself was now revealing its nature, and it seemed more powerful than any she had ever grown. The spirit of the simple was trying to speak in its own silent way, focusing on a wife by singing a song of scent. The woman had already come under its spell — but to what end?

Gothel said to the husband, "Tell me of your wife. What is her heart's desire, beyond these greens?"

The husband hemmed and hawed before blurting, "She wants to have a baby. We have tried these five long years, but still we have no child."

Gothel began thinking in the old language. "The plant is part turnip, which is *rapum*," she thought. "The woman has become *rapax*, snatching and greedy. The plants are plunder, which is *rapina*." So when the husband told about his wife's deepest desire, the pieces of the puzzle strangely came together for a moment.

"Take this *rapina*, this loot, back to your wife," said the herb woman. "Let her eat it, then plant your turnip and get her with child. If this is done her craving will be cured."

The husband did what she had told him to do, and the next day his wife was cured. When spring came, the wife gave birth to a baby girl. The husband came to Gothel's front door and told her the good news.

"Glad tidings upon your house," said Gothel, glad to see a happy end to such a bad beginning. "But be careful, rapscallion — now her womb is unlocked. Find your bliss but do not plant the turnip in the garden for a few years yet."

"Yes, yes, mother, thank you," said the husband. "We are so grateful, we named our daughter after your magic plant."

"How can that be?" said Gothel. "The mischievous simple has no name yet."

"But you told it to me, that night," said the husband. "You called it 'rapina' and that is our girl's name."

Gothel knew at once that this was a terrible name, with all sorts of bad magic about it. The spirits would hear that name spoken and they would be inspired to make cruel mischief upon the poor girl.

Scarcely ten months later, the husband's wife gave birth to twins, and the little family was in dire trouble that winter. Bad luck seemed to be following them and they blamed it upon Rapina, who had been a colicky infant. The root of their increasing misfortune was that name, since every time they said "Rapina" they attracted more bad spirits, so that by the time the twins were born there was a horde of unseen creatures surrounding the family and subjecting them to cruel jests. The husband had a wild look about him, as if he were planning to abandon the child.

This troubled Gothel. The infant was fey, since the plant was as much a parent as her mother and father. In her, the spirit of the plant had achieved human form and now it called out to the spirit world as it had once called to one woman. Gothel could see this much, and she feared for the young woman whom the infant would become. The spirits and the men they sometimes rode would take her by force, would violate her repeatedly, since that was what her name meant to them. Even worse than this was the likelihood that the offspring of such ravishment would be a terrible new race of fairy, a plague set loose upon the world.

At last Gothel came up with a plan to save the girl. She closed up her house and made ready to leave the city for another place far away, and then she offered to take Rapina with her, raising her as her own daughter. The wife wept tears of regret mixed with gratitude and finally gave the baby over.

As soon as they were away, Gothel put her face close to the baby and said, "You are Parsley. My daughter Parsley."

They went to a city in the south of France, where Gothel again practiced her trade and Parsley grew into her new name. Parsley's hair was blond and her eyes were green. She was a plain-looking child, at first, and they lived for several years in quiet happiness; but by the time she was five years old she was a pretty girl, and a few times Parsley heard a whisper when nobody was around. It surprised her, so she asked Gothel, "Mother, I heard a whispered word — what is 'Ray'?"

"It is a bad thing," said Gothel.

They moved from the city to a town. They lived there in relative comfort, but Parsley's appearance continued to improve, and by the time she was nine, she was beautiful. The whispering came again to Parsley, in moments of quiet twilight or silent night.

"Mother, I hear whispering like when I was a child," said Parsley. Gothel's eyes grew wide. "What is 'Ray-Pee'?"

"It is a very bad thing," said Gothel.

They moved again, this time to a village where they lived in poverty. Still Parsley's beauty blossomed, and when she was twelve, she was no longer simply beautiful: she was the most beautiful girl under the sun.

The mischief stormed around them. Parsley saw that Gothel now had a wild look at times. There was an evening when Parsley was tending the garden and a passing farmer stopped to say something strange to her. She looked up at him, a man she had known for years, and was frightened by his glowing eyes.

She ran crying to Gothel, who comforted her and listened to the story until Parsley asked, "Mo-mother, what is 'Ray-Pee-N —'?"

"Don't say it," cried Gothel, interrupting her. "It is a terrible thing, never to be spoken!"

The next day Gothel took Parsley into the forest to gather wild simples. In the middle of the forest they came upon a tower that had neither stairs nor doors, only a big window eighty feet above the ground.

"Child," said Gothel, "this is our new home."

They lived at the tower for years. By day, they gathered simples from garden and forest, and prepared compounds. At night, they slept in the tower. On market days, Gothel took bundles of simples and compounds to town to sell them, and during those times, Parsley was alone.

To enter and leave they used a rope ladder. As time passed, one part or another would wear. They repaired it by twisting some of Parsley's hair into the rope.

Parsley was very excited one day when Gothel came back from the market town. "Mother," she said. "A man was down there!"

"A man?" said Gothel, so surprised that she nearly fell off the ladder. "A hunter, was it?"

"He said he was a troubadour," said Parsley.

Gothel muttered at that, and then she asked, "Did he ask you to let down the ladder?"

"Yes," said Parsley.

"And did you?" asked Gothel.

"Oh, no, Mother!"

"Good girl," said Gothel, and she began climbing again.

Once Gothel was inside, Parsley told more:

"He played the lute and sang a beautiful song about a knight who met a shepherdess — 'The other day I went wandering' — that's how it began."

"What happened to her, in the song?" asked Gothel,

knowing that nine times out of ten *pastorelas* she was violated.

"She refused his advances," said Parsley with a laugh. "She hit him on the head with her crook! Then he went away, saying he hoped she would favor him one day."

The troubadour came again a few days later. Marveling at their rope ladder, he asked, "How did you manage to get up there the first time?"

"There was a string that went up around yon beam and down again," said Gothel. "We tied a rope to the string and drew it up and over the beam."

The troubadour said, "But how did you get the string up there?"

"We had a little help," said Gothel.

At first Gothel was very suspicious of him, but he answered her questions directly. He was a troubadour, well versed in the arts of courtly love.

Gothel spoke to him of the *Cathar* ideals as well as the erotic arts they were rumored to practice. She told him of "mining black earth"; she showed him the symbol of Pisces, the two fish swimming head to tail, and had him explain its significance in this context; they discussed Sodom and Gomorrah and agreed that the true sin had not been what the men did for carnal pleasure with themselves but their violation of others. She started an immoral story made immortal by Boccaccio, and he finished it. She asked whether he knew male continence; he said he did, and she believed him.

Gothel envisioned a solution to all their problems. The young couple separated from the world, with herself to help and nurture them — it would be an earthly paradise, Eden regained. There would be amorous delight but no offspring, and thus the bad seed of the mischievous simple would come to an end. After Parsley was past her child-bearing years, once age had ravaged her terrible beauty, then she could safely go out into the world as a crone and be a great herb woman, or she could live out her remaining days in the forest.

Gothel spoke to him. "As you can see, we are living here in imitation of the *stylites*, above and away from the world. Perhaps you can stay with us and we could live in the purity of the *Cathars*. Failing that lofty ideal, you and she could practice the earthy arts of the *Bogomils*. I offer you my only daughter and an earthly paradise, with only one rule — there must be no offspring. Just like the *Cathars*. Can you swear with good conscience to such a bargain?"

As he considered, she looked about his head and shoulders for signs of possession past or present, and then she looked deep into his eyes. She saw that he was human and pure of heart.

"Yes," he said. "I swear it."

The first season was a very happy time. Just knowing that Parsley was not alone while Gothel was away, made the herb woman feel more at ease on her visits to the market town. They sang *tensos*, the cerebral debate songs of love and ethics; they sang *sirventeses*, the visceral partisan songs shining with praise or oozing with vitriol. But the best was when they would sing a sweet *pastorela*, with him singing as the knight and Parsley singing as the shepherdess, followed by an alba, song of lovers in the night: "Ah God, ah God, the dawn it comes too soon . . . "

Seeing the young couple together was a delight to Gothel, and hearing them sing so sweetly together brought tears of joy to her eyes.

After spring came summer, and Gothel's heart was so full of happiness she thought it might burst. Then one morning at the end of summer, as Parsley was struggling to put on her clothes, she said, "Mother, why are my clothes getting smaller?"

Gothel glanced over at her and, as if the scales had fallen from her eyes, she could see that Parsley was with child.

"Oh, you wicked creature," cried Gothel. "You carry

another life inside you; you have broken the one rule!"

"No, no," wailed Parsley. "That is impossible! The safe days, the sign of the Pisces, the vinegar sponge, the arts *bougre* — Mother, sweet Mother, we followed the law you set down. I cannot be pregnant!"

"Alas, you are," said Gothel. She took up her knife with grim determination and said, "I should save the world by killing you now. Come here."

Trembling with fear at this dreadful change in Gothel, Parsley knelt at her feet. Gothel reached down and sliced off her long braid, which made Parsley sob.

"My Oath to Hippocrates has spared your life," said Gothel. She forced her daughter to climb down from the tower and then drove her into the wilderness.

"You were cursed before your birth," Gothel raged at Parsley as they hiked along their pathless way. "I have spent seventeen years trying to change your fate, and all for nothing. Your name will be more known than fabled Lilith or Pandora, of this I am certain, but I fear you will be remembered as mother to demons."

After many hours they came to a clearing with a few ruinous cottages used by swineherds. Gothel pointed them out and then spoke her final words to the young woman: "You walk alone henceforth. Cast yourself upon their mercy! I have no daughter, and your name is not Parsley."

As the twilight deepened toward night, the troubadour arrived at the base of the tower and whistled. The rope ladder was lowered and up he climbed, expecting to find his beloved Parsley alone. Instead, he found Gothel, sitting at the table with only a guttering candle-stub for light.

"Mother Gothel!" he said. "I thought you gone to town."

"No, not yet," she said. "But soon." Her voice was old and tired.

"But Mother Gothel, it is night now!" he said, surprised at her words.

"Yes," said Gothel, staring into her cup.

"Where is Parsley?" he asked, growing uneasy.

"She is gone," said Gothel. "She has been cast out for being with child. I trusted you, and you betrayed my trust."

"Wait — wait!" squeaked the troubadour in fright. "Isn't there a compound to remedy her condition?"

She glared at him with a baneful eye. "Yes, there is such a compound, and she knows it, too. She is an herb woman. I wash my hands of it, and you both." With that, she stood up, drank the cup, and spit its fluid into his face. He screamed as the poison blinded him. His limbs felt heavy as stone, making him fall over. He tried to rise but could not. He fainted as she worked her terrible revenge upon him, and then she left the tower forever, leaving a tribe of spirits the charge of tormenting him.

•

Parsley found a swineherd's wife who was willing to add her to the household in exchange for helping with chores and practicing her medicine. When Parsley's time came the wife helped her give birth to twins, a colicky girl with pointed ears and a quiet boy.

One night the swineherd's wife suddenly spoke in a different voice: "*Rapina.*"

Parsley saw the eerie gleam in her eye. "Who are you?"

"We watch your *troubadour* wander the forest like a wild man," said the eerie voice. "He has gone in circles for two years."

"He is still alive?" said Parsley, weeping with hope.

"Barely," was the answer. "He will die soon."

"Please bring him to me," cried Parsley.

"Would you still have him? He is blind and unmanned."

"Please!"

"We will trade him for your twins."

"What?" Her blood ran cold. "What are you saying?"

"We will give him to you if you give us your children."

"You are monsters!"

"Yes," said the voice. "And we claim the children are our own."

"No. Not my babies. No!"

"Your man will die before sunrise."

"No! This is too much."

Parsley trembled as she grappled with the horrific offer. *It is impossible*, she thought, *a devil's bargain — there is no way to win, either way.*

"Not both —" she said, the thought coming out before she could halt it. She groaned, bending over.

"Just one child?"

"I — I can't make the choice," said Parsley.

"To bargain or not?"

"No!" hissed Parsley. "Which — which child . . . "

"You know and we know which child. The girl."

Parsley began panting.

"This is your final offer," said the voice. "Take your daughter to the stream and sing as though your heart were breaking. Go now."

The glow faded from the wife's eyes and she started as if suddenly awakened. "What was I . . . ?"

Her befuddlement changed into concern as she saw Parsley's face.

"You look like you've seen a ghost! Where are you going?"

Parsley took up her sleeping daughter and ran out into the night. At the stream's side she sang a lament; she sang a *sirventes* against the cruel oppressors; she sang an alba, but at the first "Ah God, ah God, the dawn it comes too soon" she broke down in sobs.

As soon as she could breathe again, she bravely began their sweet *pastorela*: "The other day I went wandering . . . "

After a time she heard a shout and a crashing through the bushes on the other side. Then the ragged troubadour appeared there in the moonlight, and he sang his part of the song.

Parsley's heart leapt at the sight of him. He waded out into the stream. She started to go but hesitated. He stumbled as if shoved and she saw dark hands pushing his head down toward the water.

She stepped into the water and waded out to the middle. The dark hands released him and reached out for the baby.

She gave up her daughter and regained her lover.

The couple wept in their embrace. The troubadour's long beard, tangled with twigs, was wet from his near drowning.

"Parsley, forgive me," he said. "Forgive me for making you with child." He wept fresh tears of regret.

"My love, I forgive you," she said. "I have given you a son!" And then she cried her own tears of regret.

A BREEN CARNATION

The road was slick in the darkness, the bridge was narrow. The railing could not stop the skidding 4x4 truck, nor even slow it down, and as it gave way with a sound like snapping matchsticks, Todd Kingfisher felt the first intimation that he might not walk away from this crash. A radio commercial sang a Christmas jingle, the roiling waters of the swollen creek lit by the truck's headlights as the wheels went over the edge, and Todd thought of his family — his wife Rochelle, their daughter Margaret, and the baby on the way. Her green eyes, his hopes for his children, as the truck somersaulted into the water, brought short by the icy darkness of impact.

"Rochelle," he said, opening his eyes in the whiteness. He was in a bed, and the whiteness resolved into whites and greens. Was the crash a dream, or was he dead? There was an insect droning sound in the distance. He began to weep with relief as he thought, *Hospital. I'm in a hospital. That sound is a TV turned low.*

The night nurse was very happy. "We're calling your wife," she said. "She'll be here soon." He became aware of the IV drip in his arm, and the machines around the bed.

"What happened?"

"There was an accident, but you're safe now."

His wife came. Her hair was dyed red, her eyes were brown, her ears were large. Her name was Jenny.

•

It was only a momentary lapse, despite all the confusion of that first instant. There were tests, a lot of tests, measuring his motor skills and probing for possible memory loss. People were vague about the accident, but Todd quickly learned that he had been "out" for more than a few hours, perhaps more than a few days. He had a lot of questions about the accident, but in the meantime there were these tests, and he wanted to give the right answer.

Some tests were conducted by medical staff who recorded his answers, but the more subtle tests were in dealing with Jenny and Kevin, his teenage son. Paper tests were easier, black and white, cut and dry. Both tester and test-subject knew that it was a test, and the test had a beginning and an end.

The family tests were more nebulous. Jenny would probe gently, not wanting to find out that he couldn't remember something or that he was somehow damaged from the accident. Her anxiety rubbed off on him and he learned to read her subconscious cues as pointers to the right answers. He felt that he had somehow lost something, but he didn't want anyone to know, so he memorized his family as quickly as he could.

In the fullness of time they admitted to Todd that he had been "out" for a few weeks. Well, maybe several. More harrowing than that were the details of his rescue from the icy waters by paramedics, and the heart of their secret seemed to be that he was dead when they pulled him out. They showed him the video, and watching them wrestle his pale body from its watery grave in the harsh glare, he resolved to lose some weight. As a chilled corpse he had been taken to the hospital and revived with the everyday miracle of modern medicine.

Todd Kingfisher passed nearly all of the tests and was discharged from the hospital. He tried very hard to cope with the acceleration, secretly memorizing all the details of a life thrown at him, but it was an intense and tiring process. On his first day at home he was watching the news and they were covering the St. Patrick's Day festivities. There was a shot of some colored carnations, with the newscaster's commentary about the lovely breen carnations . . .

Breen?

Todd thought he had misheard it, but it came up again. Breen, breen, breen. Not what he would have called that color at all. The word "green" came to his lips, but he didn't say it. He felt his stomach tighten. Was this another *problem*, another secret to hide and digest? He tried the dictionary. There was nothing under "green," but there was an entry for "breen."

Cautiously he studied the world around him, using leading questions in what he hoped was an offhand way. The American flag was red, white, and breen. A dark-breen, that one. On St. Paddy's day people wear breen (a light-breen). A traffic light was red, yellow, and breen (a mid- to light-breen). The sky, the sea, the grass, the trees, the dollars, the jeans — all shades of breen.

There were a few other private color words in his head besides "green," but Todd locked them away as symptoms of a dream — or something much worse.

•

The breakdown came a few months later, seemingly out of the breen. Todd had managed all the hurdles of re-memorizing his family and his job as a postal worker only to find that his life was empty. There was one day when he suddenly realized that he had been miserable for weeks, living under a dark cloud of trying to fit into a mold of himself created by others. He knew all about the insurmountable rift between himself and his rebellious "son" Kevin; likewise the insatiable consumerism of his "wife" Jenny, piling up debt; the undeniable inefficiency of the post office and the barely concealed anger of the customers . . . he wanted out of it, all of it.

So he quit his job, moved into a small downtown apartment, and enrolled in classes at the community college with the goal of becoming a classical music disc jockey. Jenny wasn't happy about this sudden change and seemed convinced that it was a middle age crisis he was going through. She clung to this idea despite the angry outburst when he told her the truth as he saw it. In the stunned aftermath of that thunderclap there was vague talk of psychiatric help, mental wards, and the like, until Jenny's internal gyros righted themselves and she decided he was speaking metaphorically.

Todd felt happy for the first time, giddy with the new freedom. He had a one room apartment, with a mattress on the hardwood floor, and most of his belongings in boxes and paper bags — more primitive than his days in the college frat house. One bag nearly glowed with cryptic significance, filled with junk salvaged from his truck: insurance papers stuck together, receipts washed of their ink, roadmaps whose topography were rearranged by waterstains and wrinkles, a pressure gauge, and a paperback book.

While his spartan apartment had a radio, there was no television set (due in part, perhaps, to the rude shock the last one had given him), so for entertainment he began to read the book while listening to the classical music station.

It was *Twilight Through the Trees,* a novel by Jack Forgewood. There was a bookmark towards the end, but since Todd couldn't remember a thing about the book, he started at the beginning. The hero was a composer named Rex Fischer who was married to the lovely Rochelle (who had delicately shaped ears and eyes as breen as apples), and they had a daughter named Margaret . . .

Todd vomited into the toilet, then curled into a ball, shivering as he broke out in a body sweat.

Okay, Todd, he thought. *Reality check. There's a simple answer to this — you were reading that book before the crash, and you mixed it up with your life. This doesn't mean that your move to work in radio is related to Rex's profession. Fact is fact and fiction is fiction. You are alive and Rex never really lived at all, except as a dream. Even if your dissatisfaction with your old life was based upon a misunderstanding of fiction as fact, still, you wanted — needed — to get out of that situation. It was living a lie.*

But still. Rex was the one who had belonged to a fraternity. Todd never had.

•

It was like a nagging toothache, or trying not to think about pink elephants. Steeling himself, he read the novel through to its more-or-less happy ending, an ending that gave him an odd sense of hope. He wrote a letter to the author Jack Forgewood in care of the publishers, a letter that mentioned nothing about the strange circumstances, just that he had been deeply impressed by the novel. That done, he tried to concentrate on his schoolwork.

Seven weeks later he got a letter from Jack Forgewood. It was a friendly reply to fan mail. Forgewood had a post office box in a small town only a few hundred miles away. On a giddy impulse, Todd set out the next morning in his used car.

•

The town was similar in many ways to the town in *Twilight Through the Trees.* Not exactly the same, but there were little details — an old fashioned diner next to the post office seemed especially significant. While lunching on a French dip sandwich, he asked the waitress about Forgewood and learned that he did stop in from time to time, often at lunchtime, but not that day.

The public library had a complete collection of Forgewood's work, a dozen novels and two books of short stories. Todd studied the author photos, read the jacket blurbs. *Twilight Through the Trees,* originally published twenty years before, was apparently not considered one of his best works.

The next morning found Todd sitting on a park bench on the town square, reading the local paper, watching the post office, and beginning to have second thoughts.

This is kind of crazy. What am I doing? Mail delivered by eleven o'clock, that's what the sign said. Maybe he'll come earlier, since he didn't come yesterday? Well, he might *have come yesterday. Okay, this is crazy. If he's not here by noon, I'll go home.*

Autumn was more advanced here; the leaves had already turned and fallen. He read the personals. *Who are these people? What are their stories?*

•

"Uh, Mister Forgewood?"

"Yes?" The man looked up from his handful of letters, standing outside the post office. He looked very much like the dust jacket photos: the white hair, the widow's peak, the eyes wide to the point of bulging.

"Hello, I'm Todd Kingfisher. I'm a big fan of yours — I wrote you a letter a while back?" He offered his hand. "It's a great honor to meet you, sir. Would you, ah, sign my book?"

Forgewood's smile turned puzzled as he saw the ragged paperback.

"It's, ah, seen better days, but it is very dear to me."

"Sure, I understand," said Forgewood, getting out his pen. "Kingfisher, eh? Seems like I just sent you a letter the other day."

"Yes, yes you did, and I just happened to be up here in

your neck of the woods — for a few more hours . . . oh, thank you very much. It means a great deal to me. Listen, can I buy you lunch, or a cup of coffee or something?"

Forgewood started to frown, but then he glanced at the bills and junk mail in his hand. He shrugged. "Okay, why not?" He smiled.

They sat at the counter and ordered coffee. Todd put the book on the counter top.

"Yeah, this book and I have gone through a lot together. See how waterlogged it has been? Well, almost a year ago I crashed my car . . ."

So Todd told his story in bits and pieces, not looking at Forgewood for fear and shame. But after he had finished, he did steal a glance to find Forgewood in a sort of reverie.

"Secrets being buried deeper every day," the older man said softly as the waitress refilled his coffee cup. "Both are true, based on careful psychological evaluations." He turned to Todd. "The first is that superstition is good for you. Superstitious people are happier and more successful. The second is that optimism is good for you — even unjustified optimism. Optimistic people are healthier and do better work."

"I don't understand . . . ."

"That was an interesting story you told," said Forgewood. "Now let me tell one. There was once a fellow, living on the coast, and he had these artistic ambitions. Wanted to create things, share the worlds cluttering up his head with other people, total strangers. But he was plagued by unruly emotions, 'manic-depressive' as they used to say — on good days he was ready to save the world, but on bad days he was ready to shoot himself. And on one very bad day, he did. He put a bullet in his brain.

"But here's the thing — he didn't die. The caliber was small, but still, it was something of a miracle. Not just that he was still alive, but that the bullet had destroyed the depressive section of his brain. The doctors tested him and declared it so, and the man really couldn't fathom trying to kill himself anymore. It was written up in newspapers and medical journals as the most extraordinary case of successful radical neurosurgery ever documented. And yet, someone *did* die, didn't he? Didn't his depressive self actually get the suicide he wanted?

"There were some complications, not mentioned in any of the articles about this case . . . let's see, how shall we do this? Ah, yes."

Forgewood scribbled something on the back of a junk mail envelope, then put it down on the counter, face up.

"Now then, you mentioned that you had a certain aphasia related to color, but you didn't tell me what color or colors they were, or the unusual names that you gave them. Please use them now, and tell me: what is the color of the sky?"

"Blue," said Todd, his tongue suddenly thick.

"And what is the color of grass?"

"G-green," he stammered.

"And the sun? What color is that?"

Todd blinked with surprise.

"Yellow?"

Forgewood barked a laugh and slapped the counter. He turned over the envelope, saying, "Here you go."

Todd read the list: *blue, green, gelo.*

"Two out of three, not bad," said Forgewood.

"But what does it mean?"

"Who knows? Maybe nothing. I could be lying. You could be lying. We both could be lying. But don't forget what I told you about superstition and optimism. And there *is* cause for optimism."

"Wait," said Todd. "You mean . . . I'm not —?"

"The first?" said Forgewood. "No, Rex, you're not."

•

There is more than one mundane reality: the cook and the busboy have different impressions of the same meal served at the restaurant; the salaryman in the metropolis and the neolithic tribesman in the rainforest have different ideas of the same planet that they both live on. In addition there may be more than one universe. In the world Todd remembered as living in before, a writer was assumed to base characters upon personally known people. But here, in this strange new place, it seemed that causality was reversed for at least one writer, so that pure fiction became, through time and consequence, solid fact.

Did the writer summon them from their old place or places to this new place, or did he only announce their arrivals ahead of time as one might look at a train schedule?

•

Rochelle, I hope the message of this story gets to you. I've blurred some of the details to protect us all, but you should be able to piece it together, especially through the book I've referred to as "Twilight Through the Trees." You will have gone through some kind of serious medical trauma, and certain things will be "not quite right." You will be able to figure out the location of the town, I'm sure. I'm living there now, working at the local radio station, waiting for the divorce to come through.

Write when you get this. Call me when you get here.

HITLER'S HOLLYWOOD

Leni licked her lips, then snapped open her compact and checked her lipstick for the fourth time. Even in the audience seats, far away from the stage lights, the air seemed hot, stifling, as if someone had pumped away the oxygen.

It was a capacity crowd in the cinema at Festival de Cannes, the gentlemen somber in their dark evening wear, the ladies dazzling in their beautiful gowns. Leni and Rita sat together in the fifth row near the aisle, surrounded by ten SS officers disguised as glitterati. The two women might have been a mother and her middle-aged daughter: Leni was sixty years old, her hair a convincing blonde, and Rita was in her forties, her auburn-dyed tresses pinned up.

This is worse than in '35, Leni thought. *I'm acting like a child. Realistically, how bad could it be? Say it ends my career, but I should retire, anyway. I wouldn't be 'disappeared,' would I? Piano-wire garrote? I could live through the shame but not an execution.*

She smothered a hysterical giggle.

Rita began fidgeting. Leni attended to her at once, producing a candy from her clutch.

"Rita?" whispered Leni. "Remember what I said? Have this."

Rita greedily ate the bourbon-filled bonbon, then looked around with restored serenity.

The lights dimmed. The stage curtains parted to reveal the movie screen. The master of ceremonies emerged from stage left and crossed to the podium at stage right.

"Bonsoir mesdames and messieurs, and welcome to the Grand Theatre Lumiere," he said. "Nineteen sixty-three will be remembered as the year when fascism saved Europe by destroying Bolshevism. The future promised decades ago has finally come: Europe is united and at peace, from Lisbon to the Urals, from Sicily to Iceland. The dream of the Fuhrer and Petain has been brought to fruition.

"Tonight it may seem foreordained that there be a united Europe, but in the heroic struggle across two world wars, victory was anything but certain. Yet even in the blackest hour of 1944 there was a shining beacon of hope: the actress we honor tonight, Rita Hayworth."

The lights dimmed to darkness as he stepped away.

The documentary began with blackness and the swirling magic at the beginning of Wagner's *Ride of the Valkyries*. With the trumpeted melody came a series of black and white stills arranged side by side. Each showed Rita as a different character in a signature scene, starting with day nurse Pauline, followed by cabaret singer Gilda, cub reporter Kimberly, freedom fighter Jane, and army nurse Hot Lips. The title, *Goddess of Love & War*, came down from the top to blaze above the stills. The subtitle, *the Five Faces of Rita*, rose up from the bottom.

The title screen dissolved to the scene of *Johnny Got His Gun* (1939) where the young day nurse Pauline, in white uniform and wimple, leans forward at the bedside of the mangled British soldier. Her eyes full of heartbreaking pity, she says, "Merry Christmas, Mr. Bonham," as she writes this message on the invalid's chest with her finger.

•

The film clip stirred Margarita's memories of the party at San Simeon where *Johnny Got His Gun* had been given a prerelease showing in the private theater. William Randolph Hearst, lord of the castle, had seemed very enthusiastic about the movie. She was there again, feeling as bubbly as the champagne she sipped; her career had begun, and her new life stretched out before her to a golden horizon.

From across the room of Hollywood's movers and shakers she saw Orson. He was young, with a cherubic face, and new to Hollywood just like she was, but he was tall, and so powerful that she could feel waves of electricity coming off of him, even at a distance. As he drew closer with Joe Cotton she felt herself light up from inside, from something more than just the champagne.

"Orson, this is Rita," said Joe.

"Rita, I was just giving Joe here a mini-lecture," said Orson, taking her hand. "About how Europe is sick with three diseases: the Red, the Black, and the Pink."

"The Pink?" she asked.

"Socialism," he said. "America should have nothing to do with this war. Already people are forgetting the horrors of the Great War, even the Mustard Gas of Ypres and the hell of Verdun. Which is why your movie is so important, they must be reminded."

"Well it isn't really *my* movie . . ." she said, attracted to his power.

"Ah, but it is," said Orson, warmly, confidently. "You have made it your own. Now that war has started in Europe, America will be suckered into it once again. I predict it will run for four years, just as it did the last time. It's like a murderous game of football where at half-time America comes in and takes heavy losses for the Europeans. You can see how this will go — FDR will try and get us in by '42."

"Orson is a solid FDR man," said Joe with a grin. "Or at least he was, until he saw your movie!"

"I am still for FDR," said Orson, a little reproachfully. "I only fear that he will not keep his promise to keep us out of war."

"But won't there be a lasting peace after this war?" asked Margarita, falling into the role of an eager student.

"No more than the one following the 'War to End All War,'" said Orson. "There will be another fourteen year festering period until the third war starts around 1959, and that one will run for another four years."

"Why can't it go longer than four years?" asked Rita. "That movie *Things to Come* has it running for decades."

"Exhaustion," said Orson. "Materials are used up, soldiers are killed, and society becomes tired of the whole mess. At five years the game is in overtime; it simply can't last six years, and America cannot stomach more than two years of it."

"So is there a fourth war in the '70s?"

"Yes, the cycle keeps repeating until the Europeans learn to stop fighting. Well, they have their four-year plans, and I have mine."

•

The documentary cut to a color interview of middle-aged Rita, sitting on a leather couch in the elegant living room of a European apartment. She was as beautiful and as poised as ever.

"*Johnny Got His Gun* was your first acting role," said Leni, off-camera.

"Yes." Rita's response was a little wooden, which made Leni in the audience wince. She remembered meeting the "goddess" in 1961, and how she had discovered a woman so wrecked by severe alcoholism that she seemed prematurely senile at times and demented at others.

"Your look for that movie was fresh and pure, very virginal with the starched white nurse's uniform."

"Yes." Rather than wooden, it was now unmistakably

the demure quality of day nurse Pauline.

"But very sexy in that sort of way."

"If you say so."

"Your part wasn't very big but you stole the show," said Leni. "People took to calling the movie 'Merry Christmas, Mr. Bonham.'"

"Did they?" A big "Kimberly" smile, sexy but not incandescent. "I didn't know that."

"Your next film was *The Message of Dunkirk*," said Leni. "In your first starring role you played Gilda, a cabaret dancer who falls in love with a British soldier during the Phony War."

"Yes."

Cut to a clip of *The Message of Dunkirk* (1940), where Gilda is in her dressing room at the cabaret. A man's voice calls through the door, "Gilda, are you decent?"

She tosses her hair, looks straight into the camera and says, with mock innocence, "Who, me?"

Cut to a muted scene of the "officer's club" cabaret, where Gilda, in strapless evening gown and long gloves, sings "Put the Blame on Mame" while performing a near strip tease.

In voice over, Leni said, "You had training at dance, you were a dancer before becoming an actress, and your husband the director wisely showcased your talents."

Gilda tosses her hair, she raises her arms above her head, she peels off a long glove and throws it into the ecstatic audience, an action that set the cinema world on fire.

"This movie established you as a sex goddess at the age of twenty-two," said Leni. "But there was a more serious note to it, best summed up in this scene near the end."

Cut to the dock scene, where long lines of British soldiers are waiting to board the last boats to Great Britain.

"Don't you see, Tommy?" says Gilda, trying to reason with her boyfriend before he steps onboard. "The fighting has stopped! Mr. Hitler could have killed you all, in fact many of his generals wanted that, yet instead he offers an overture to peace."

"It wasn't his choice, it was just the weather," says Tommy. "It was a miracle."

"The gift of ten days to evacuate wasn't a *miracle*, it was a *message*," says Gilda. "Darling, you know the British treaty with Poland was silly, but you fulfilled it and were soundly beaten on the battlefield. Your honor is preserved! Simply declare peace and put the whole sorry episode behind you."

•

Seeing the film clip triggered a cascade of memories for Rita . . .

"Margarita, you and I aren't heroes," said Orson. Sipping local wine, they watched the sunset from their hotel balcony in Lisbon, a peaceful part of Europe in February 1941. "The world doesn't make any heroes outside of movies. But if Hess can meet our people in Britain, I'm certain he can make peace — you heard what he said, Hitler doesn't want to fight Britain. It would make Hearst so happy!"

"Heroes of the Peace," she said, toasting him. She loved to see him happy and this Hope tasted so good she felt they really could save America from deadly folly.

"The Pinks arrested Hess!" said Orson, waving the morning newspaper as he stormed into the bedroom of their Hollywood mansion. "It's the Great War all over again. FDR will somehow trick Congress into declaring war next year."

"Don't be so gloomy," said Margarita, nursing a hangover. "You sound like Willkie when he said FDR would get us in by April if he won re-election."

"That's a point," he said, sitting on the bed. "It didn't happen last month. And it's not going to happen, say, next month, unless they sink the *Lusitania* or something equally stupid."

"History doesn't repeat itself like that, does it?" she asked, fighting the uneasy feeling of ground giving away beneath her feet.

"Willkie was only eight months off," said Orson. "I bet he is as surprised as the rest of us!"

The Christmas decorations seemed unbearably cheery now. Margarita wanted to tear them down and go into mourning.

"God damn it, I was right," said Orson, pounding his fist into his palm. "I was right! How I wish I'd been wrong."

"Japan attacked, so we are at war with them," said Margarita. "But why get involved in Europe?"

"Because Hitler declared war on America."

"I know that, dummy, but why would he do such a thing? It was just a stupid treaty, like the one that Britain had with Poland."

"Yes, but now Hitler can sink the 'civilian' cargo ships supplying the Pinks," said Orson. "The big lie of 'American Neutrality' has finally been exposed. The timetable has been disrupted — maybe the war will end sooner because of it."

"But a war in Asia and a war in Europe . . . " said Margarita. "Can two wars be fought at the same time?"

"Probably not," said Orson, musing for a moment. "But now the timer is running and America can only last two years. Gird up your loins, woman! Throw away despair. Now we begin!"

•

The documentary cut to Rita on the couch.

"In *California Gulag* you played Kimberly Wood, a lady reporter who stumbles upon a government conspiracy to kill all Japanese Americans," said Leni. "The title itself was a slap against the unnatural American-Soviet alliance — America had entered the war at that point and the people had war-fever for most of the year until your film arrived, seemingly ripped fresh from the headlines."

"Yes," said Rita with a frown. "FDR had promised not to send our boys out to foreign wars, but he had been quietly working to do it anyway."

Cut to scene from *California Gulag* (1942): the busy newsroom of a major newspaper in Los Angeles, a cluttered landscape of roll top desks, jangling telephones, and clouds of cigarette smoke. Kimberly's boss, the crusty old editor, is trying to get her to kill the story of what she had seen at the relocation camp of Manzanar.

"You're better off doing the softer stuff, pieces on animals and children," he says.

"He got it on film!" says Kimberly, big-eyed with naive enthusiasm. "Those are American citizens —"

"They're Japs," says the editor. "It is for their own protection."

"But they're being beaten!"

"Don't worry your pretty little head over it."

Back to Rita on the couch, where Leni said, "It seems as though your influence was taking hold in America. Within a few months of *Gulag*'s release, the newspapers began to expose all the unsavory details about FDR."

"The newspapers had always hated FDR," said Rita.

"Still, it was as though a dam had been broken. By 1943 such taboo topics as his wheelchair, his mistress, and even his involvement in the assassination of Huey Long were suddenly being heard in the court of public opinion. When allegations arose that FDR had known in advance about the Pearl Harbor attack, enthusiasm for the war entered a downturn from which it never recovered."

"It was a bad war," said Rita. "FDR had been elected to keep us out of it."

"Speaking of your effort to halt the American war machine, did you really invent the Peace Sign?"

"Yes," she said with a big, sexy, Gilda laugh, tossing her hair just so. "Well, it already existed. I just borrowed it."

"How did that come about?"

"Oh, Churchill started that V-for-Victory gesture, and it looked obscene. That's where it got its power — people are like naughty school children that way. That was in '41, early in '41."

"The gesture, a fist with the thumb poking between first and middle finger, is called The Fig."

"Yes, that's right. We didn't have it in America, but we were on location in Lisbon where it is a good luck charm."

•

"Cut," said Leni. "Stay in character, Margarita. Remember, you are Rita Hitler. We'll take it again from 'Did you really invent —'"

"I don't like this," said Margarita.

"Please, do it for the doctor and he will give you a treat."

•

"— on vacation in Lisbon where it is a good luck charm," said Rita on the couch.

"In Northern Europe it is a sexy 'come hither' sort of gesture —"

"But in France it is a sexual insult," said Rita. "So we started using it at our peace rallies — we called it the Raised Fig or Fig Fist, since you have to hold it high, over your head, but everybody knows it as the Peace Sign after '42 or '43."

"Growing numbers of Americans were becoming tired of war in 1943, and your next film, *The Hidden Face*, showed the common atrocities of war hidden behind the official propaganda."

"We wanted to destroy the myth of 'liberated peoples' offering flowers to their invaders," said Rita.

"Your character, Jane Ballou, is a school teacher of coastal France," said Leni. "When her civilian husband is murdered and she is brutally raped by invading American soldiers the Valkyrie spirit awakens within her, turning her into a guerrilla fighter against the D-Day invaders. In such a controversial movie as this, the rape scene itself was actually second to this one:"

Cut to scene from *The Hidden Face* (1943) where guerrilla Jane is bringing ammunition to the German anti-aircraft gun when an American fighter plane strafes the area. Jane throws herself to the ground, hugging her German helmet to her head in terror. Looking up after the plane swoops by, she sees that her friend manning the gun has been killed.

In close up her face projects fear, then anger, and finally a steely resolve. She runs to the gun, pulls the corpse out of the way, and sits in the chair.

As the fighter plane begins another strafing run, Jane cranks the gun around into position. Bullets kick up dirt in a line heading toward her — she pulls the trigger and sees the plane burst into flames.

"The most stirring scene was at the end," said Leni. "The modern Joan of Arc's last words before the firing squad."

Cut to the scene where Jane stands tall before a brick wall pocked with bullet holes and splattered with blood. Her hands are tied behind her but she had refused a blindfold.

"FDR will never be able to break our spirit," she says. "He'll never be able to turn France, north and south, into an Anglo Saxon colony by bombing, by invading, by attacking in any way. One has only to go into the countryside and listen to the peasants describe the lives they led before the Petain revolution to understand why every bomb that is dropped only strengthens their determination to resist."

Back to Rita on the couch, composed and in color.

"It is stunning that this film accurately predicted an invasion at Normandy, nine months before it happened!" said Leni. "How did this come about?"

"That was Orson again," said Rita. "At first he wanted it to be ambiguous as to whether it was taking place in Normandy or here in France. But then he decided that Normandy was more likely, and history obliged him."

"From the distance of nearly twenty years it seems to many that Hollywood was monolithic in its anti-war stance," said Leni's voice. "But Hollywood was not entirely anti-war, was it?"

"Oh no," said Rita. "The B-studios like Republic Pictures were mainly government stooges — all those John Wayne movies, for example, and look what happened to him. RKO was one of the Big 5 studios but they became notorious for cranking out pro-government propaganda."

"For your next movie you were a nurse again, in a sense reprising your role in *Johnny Got His Gun*, but with a difference. Following the dictate that 'the first time is a tragedy, the second time is a comedy,' the film *Catch-18* was an uproariously funny black comedy."

•

Margarita closed her eyes to the clips and remembered the film's nebulous conception.

"Damn, I wish we could've gotten 'A Light in France,'" said Orson. "I would've starred and directed — just think, a gangster who fakes his own death, the possibilities . . . "

"I know, darling." The gin tasted a little oily, giving her a twinge of revulsion.

They were at the dinner table, eating the best the black market had to offer.

"But Runyon turned into another government stooge,"

said Orson. "He wants to do it as a pro-war film now."

"What about Orwell's *Catalonia*?"

"Too late, too late," said Orson. "It is already 'historical' and we need 'contemporary.' The lesson for us is that we must get the material sooner. Get the script before the novel is written. We've got a fan over there right now, flying bombers over Europe, and he's wised up to the absurdities. Might be another Sam Fuller. His writing is rough, raw, but terribly funny."

"Funny?" said Rita, putting down her fork. "You want to make a comedy about war?"

"What else can we do? We can't make *Hidden Face* again — leave that to others. No, Novelty demands we do something different."

"But a comedy!" She felt a sick knot in her stomach. "That goes against everything —"

"Finally, in the end, we have to laugh at it. We rob it of its power. Laughter is the best medicine. And you, my dearest, are a natural comedienne, as the world will soon find out!"

•

Back to Rita on the couch.

"By that time, the summer of 1944, the European theater of the war had collapsed after five years of fighting," said Leni. "D-Day had failed, which allowed a second Nazi-Soviet pact, and caused governments to fall in both Britain and America."

"D-Day was a quagmire."

"One that was eerily predicted by *Hidden Face*."

•

Margarita belatedly realized the documentary had finished and the lights were on when the master of ceremonies appeared again.

"Presenting the special award is the Fuhrer and Chancellor of Greater Germany, Adolf Hitler," he said.

The audience stood as the Great Man appeared on the stage. He shuffled to the podium, looking older than his seventy-three years. He seemed almost spent.

"Good evening," Hitler said softly. "Please sit down, thank you."

"I am pleased to be here tonight, and honored as well. I have always loved film, drawn to the dream it projects around the world, over boundaries and across borders. *King Kong* and *Snow White*, of course, but prophetic films like *Things to Come* truly moved me. I saw the power of this dream, but I was not alone. Even Stalin said, 'If I had Hollywood, I could rule the world.'"

•

"We were never pro-fascist," said Orson. "We have always been anti-war. Against American involvement in overseas fratricide, that's pro-American! I don't care what Orwell said beyond the grave — I'm shocked that he had not wised up after Catalonia, that he couldn't see the utter futility of war."

"They are only saying things, making things up," she said.

"By heaven, I saw my handkerchief in his hand!" says Orson in blackface, his hair a mass of curls, in the Venetian bedroom. "O perjured woman! thou dost stone my heart, and mak'st me call what I intend to do a murder, which I thought a sacrifice. I saw the handkerchief."

"He found it then, I never gave it him," she says. "Send for him hither. Let him confess a truth."

"He hath confessed."

"What, my lord?"

"That he hath used thee."

"How? Unlawfully?"

"Aye."

"He will not say so."

"No, his mouth is stopped. Honest Iago hath ta'en order for't."

•

"Rita Hayworth and Leni Riefenstahl, please join me on stage."

The two women stood and walked down the aisle, Leni steeling herself for the real show. For an instant it felt as though she were delivering her own daughter to the bedchamber of the girl's father.

Adolf has always had a passion for actresses, she thought. *Many of them killed themselves. But not me. Still, Rita could almost be our daughter . . .*

•

"Like Othello's last line," said heavy Orson, deep in his cups. "'Then you must speak of one that loved not wisely, but too well; of one not easily jealous, but, being wrought, perplexed in the extreme; of one whose hand, like the base Judean, threw a pearl away richer than all his tribe . . . '"

"What are you saying?" said Margarita. "You're just blue."

"I'm not sad, I'm angry!" thundered Orson. "Orwell was right — we were duped! We were starry-eyed idealists, led like sheep by our 'gentle' Nazi shepherds. In *Catalonia* he has that line about 'asking the wrong question,' something like, 'between the wars you were hooted at in left-wing circles if you suggested that Germany bore even a *fraction* of responsibility for the Great War, yet no one ever asked what would have happened if Germany had won.'"

"Probably wouldn't have made much difference at all," said Margarita.

She turned to pour another drink and finds herself standing at the bar in the cantina. They are in Spain, shooting *Touch of Evil*, set in the crime-infested California border: the decadent and decaying America that the Europeans love to see in their movies.

I'm in Hell, she thinks. *I have to save Orson. Rescue him from his darkness, bring him back up to Earth.*

"Come on, read my fortune to me," says Orson, corpulent and oozing corruption as a dirty cop.

"You haven't any," she says, frightened by this fake Tijuana that seems so real: the heat, the dust, the sweaty men, and more. Her 1957 meets her 1931, where she is thirteen years old and recently deflowered.

"What do you mean?"

The tequila bottles are filled with water, but they still have a trace scent that makes her gag.

"Your fortune isn't really all used up, Orson —" says Margarita.

"Cut!" he says. "God damn it. Come on, Rita!"

"I'm sorry," she says. "I don't think you know how hard this is for me."

"All right, take a break," he says. To the others he says, "Leave this camera here, let's pick up that 'idealist' scene over there."

"No, I can do it right this time!" she says.

"You sure?"

"Yes."

"All right," he says after an appraising look into her eyes. "Camera, sound, and . . . action.

"Come on, read my fortune to me," he says, goading the gypsy.

"You haven't any," she says dismissively. She belts down a shot of tequila.

"What do you mean?" he asks with a bit of genuine surprise.

"Your fortune is all used up," she says, a gypsy speaking doom.

"Cut. Print." He smiles at her and she feels that warm rush, a glimpse of old times.

Things will get better again, she thinks. *Thank God I don't have to dance here. I want to run away.*

"Look out," says Orson in the next shot. "Vargas'll turn you into one of these here starry-eyed idealists. They're the ones making all the real trouble in the world. Be careful, they're worse than crooks. You can always do something with a crook."

•

"Here they are," said Hitler, "my two Valkyries." He seemed to be standing straighter, and his eyes were bright.

•

"I thought it would be a stalemate, a return to the status quo, like the end of the Great War," said Orson in their last conversation. His famous voice was weak and short of breath. "That Europe would move toward a federation through treaty instead of by conquest."

"It could still happen, darling."

"No, no. World War Three is coming and it will be an apocalypse like — like a Martian Invasion." He laughed and then coughed in agony for a minute.

"Ah, *The War of the Worlds*," he said, his voice little more than a whisper. "The panic caused by the broadcast caught me by surprise, but I began to see how *War of the Worlds* was a kind of code for 'World War.' Nobody wanted another European meat-grinder, yet people could feel it coming. Could I use my genius for peace rather than just mischief?

"Then again, I thought I was a genius. A genius! And you, my love, are losing your memory even faster than I am losing my . . . illusions. What is to become of us?"

"Everything will be fine."

"When I saw you in *Johnny Got His Gun*, that is where it began. I was Mercury, you were Venus . . . together we could stop Mars, the god of war. In San Simeon."

"*In Xanadu*," she said, close to tears.

"They got me, Margarita. The Germans. This . . . disease . . . sudden and unknown, it might be poison. A medical weapon. Revenge of the Martians."

"Hush, you'll be fine!"

"But they won't touch you, my sweet," he gasped. "Give my love to Hearst and . . . Rosebud . . . "

·

This can't be happening, she thinks in a cold sweat. *I've got to do something. I've got to take it all back.*

She finds herself drenched, naked, and alone, laughed at by an audience of cruel gods. She turns and runs from the Mediterranean sun into the closed part of the shower tent, where she throws on the bathrobe lying there.

She runs out of the tent and into the Normandy Invasion, where she pauses only to shoot the German soldier working the anti-aircraft gun.

She runs to the newsroom in Los Angeles, where she tells the editor, "You're right, this Manzanar camp really isn't much of a story compared to Eastern Europe."

She runs to the dock of Dunkirk and tells her soldier beau Tommy, "Live to fight another day, but don't give up the fight. Free Poland!"

She runs to the hospital bed and showers mangled Johnny with tears as she writes on his chest: "Thank you, thank you, thank you."

She runs, exhausted, into a lurid wasteland, where the smoldering ruins of a once fair city stretch out to a horizon marked by a ring of mushroom clouds. The choking smell of countless corpses, soldiers and civilians, adults and children: the world turned into a burning charnel pit. It is Red Poland, 1962; it is *Things to Come*, a movie she saw as a girl in 1936; it is both.

The rocket man will come soon, she thinks, scanning the air.

A man with white hair, wearing a black suit. All will be better then.

•

"On behalf of Europe, please accept this medal," said Hitler. "Mussolini had his famous fifth column, but I was lucky enough to have Hollywood, an army with you at its head."

"Armies have marched over me," said Rita to the rocket man.

Leni was startled but she remained composed, recognizing it as another movie quote.

This is it, she thought. *A personal triumph of will if I can make it through this.*

"Indeed!" said Hitler.

"But, Mr. Hitler, why did you declare war on America?"

Leni blanched and saw stars swimming at the edge of her vision. People had been 'disappeared' for such things.

"To you I must confess it was a mistake," said Hitler. The theatre was so silent one might hear a pin drop. "The treaty with Japan was silly, but I fulfilled it . . . "

"Your honor is preserved!" said Rita. "Simply declare peace and put the whole sorry episode behind you."

"Exactly," said Hitler, nodding. "And so we did. It is easier now that America and China have eliminated Bolshevism in the Far East during our atomkrieg."

"'The enemy of my enemy is my friend.'"

"Just so," said Hitler with a small smile. "And now, Rita Hayworth —"

"Rita *Hitler*," said Rita.

Leni gasped and the audience murmured, but Hitler lit up, shedding decades of apparent age. Power radiated from him in waves.

"Immortal Rita, please allow me to put this necklace on you."

"Yes, thank you," she said, demure as Pauline. The

room held its breath as Hitler's hands went around the neck of the most beautiful woman in the world.

After he put it on her, she coquetted by reaching up, unpinning her hair, and shaking it out as incandescent Gilda.

A man in the front row jumped up and shouted, "Sieg—"

The room surged into a standing ovation.

"Heil! Sieg Heil! Sieg Heil!"

Leni beamed with pride and relief. At least Rita had gotten *that* part right.

AMONG THE SHATTERED
AND DEBRIS

5. The Beginning (2050)

There are moments of personal change in which it seems the world itself has been transformed. When Dean Gray went away to college, he arrived there as a new man in a new world. He felt his life was finally getting started, breaking from a dark cocoon. He could taste electricity in the air at the San Francisco campus, and for the first time he had a direction of his own choosing. The little geek, the neighborhood whipping boy, the book-reading nerd was finally up on the track to success in the booming field of Nanotech, where he would be accepted for his brains, rather than being reviled for his lack of brawn.

He first met Meg in one of those freshman requirement courses.

"So, what's your major?" he asked, trying to sound casual.

"Singularity Studies," she said like a challenge, friendly yet guarded.

"Oo, that's deep . . . " he said, trying to be diplomatic about that failed dream of the previous generation. According to the Singularity futurists, by 2030 a Seed A.I. would awaken to self-consciousness and transform the world overnight, a technological leap so profound as to be a Singularity. Supposedly the human era would end shortly thereafter, replaced by an era of post-humans and/or transhumans. Some people clung to Singularity theory like a religion, even after the collapse of the Seed A.I. bubble in 2027.

". . . but completely impractical, as my boyfriend likes to say."

That was the signal for Dean to turn and run away. But there was something about Meg that attracted him, and he endured months of sweet anguish, his old victimized side telling him that she was outside of his league, while his new heroic side sang that he loved her more than anybody else could.

4. The Ring (2054)

Dean paced around their apartment, the diamond ring burning in his hand.

This will be the day it all comes right. All my suffering in life was down payment. I'm a new person and life will be good from here on out if you will be with me, Meg.

He knew it would be better to build the mood, set the scene with dinner at a nice restaurant. *We aren't poor students anymore. I've got the killer job, like I'm strapped to a rocket that's blasting off.* But he could not bear to up the ante any further or chance a rejection in such a public place.

Hearing the key enter the lock, he rushed over and opened the door to find Meg encumbered with grocery bags.

"Oh, you're home!" she said. "Here —"

She expected him to take a bag but he went down on one knee, there in the doorway.

"Please marry me, Meg," he said.

She took a breath to laugh but she saw the velvet box with the ring and it caught in her throat, there in the doorway with her keychain swinging against the door and the ice cream box sweating.

Her face, her smile, and a world of bright promise. It was heaven, it was a personal Singularity he passed through, to find himself a changed person in a changed world.

3. The Mesh (2054)

The wire technology was just taking off when they got married.

"The basic mesh has replaced the cell phone, the laptop computer, and the headset in India," said the pink-faced surgeon, giving them the spiel in his suite. "Overnight the mesh became indispensable to the workforce over there, and Heal-US has just given the green light for domestic installation."

"But what does it do?" said Dean, trying to break the infomercial or at least cut it short.

"There are two modes — Work mode, which gives instant access to teammates, and Spouse mode, which gives a deeper link between spouses. It is a technological telepathy."

"There are also executive models?" asked Dean, trying not to stare at the surgeon's long nose and pointy chin.

"Yes, they are experimental right now, but if you can get a voucher . . . "

"Dean was nominated for an executive wire," said Meg, beaming with pride.

"Well, congratulations!" said the surgeon, sweeping a hand at his receding hairline and giving Dean a look of reappraisal. "That seems like a big vote of confidence."

"Practically a promotion in itself," said Meg.

"So, what is different about the model?"

"With this one you have a third mode, the command mode, that can access a mesh directly, without the wearer's permission. Rather than text or audio messages, it broadcasts feelings, a bit like the Spouse mode but active rather than passive, and the range is limited. The idea was to go beyond telepathy and create a tel-*empathy* device."

Dean and Meg had the wires installed so that they were always connected even when apart and could see each other's thoughts as their own. That was when he saw her side.

You don't love me as much, but that's okay. This is the thing that is going to save me. This is the mast that I'll tie myself to.

2. The Baby (2055)

A series of steps — the job, the wife, the house, and then the baby. The best job, the best wife, the best house, the perfect baby. Life Is Good, Life Has Begun.

But it was hard to be a parent, and the baby was sick, which is scary and expensive. Meg grew resentful being left at home with the baby, but Dean persevered, thinking, *we can work this out, we can make this work, this is the thing that's going to save me.*

Then the nanotech industry imploded, taking Dean's job, his house, and his marriage. When Meg disconnected, Dean felt cut in half, left blinded and crippled at the trash heap. Quickly she wired with Bob, that scion of old h2 money, living in a big mansion with maids, a cook, a nanny, and the best foreign treatment that money could buy for Allie.

1. The Singer (2056)

In his new role, Dean would glide into the watering hole like he was just another mesh-implanted drone. There, among the customers supposedly on break but with their data glasses still on, texting with thumbs on their finger segments, working as they ingested short term stimulants and performance enhancers, he would broadcast in ways that juiced their flow and fluttered their breath. He was rare, a wi-fi gigolo, always anonymous.

He entered, he entertained, he exited.

A blue collar bistro serving data clerks freed from their

cubicles to get a tofu worldwrap and a cup of chai. Dean would play for them the Work Song, taping into his best memories of purpose, the workday bounded by the home time, the loving wife and the infant.

At a white collar cafe of managers he might broadcast the Bright Future Overture, and they felt his old college hope, his former anticipation of good things coming soon.

In a green collar establishment where the executives gathered he shaded the Love song "He doesn't love you like I love you," the heady emotions he had felt when he finally told Meg, into a tantalizing appetizer for mergers and acquisitions.

All delivered directly to their emotional receptors in a manner world-weary, fate-battered, and slightly jaded. Like sensing the bruised heart of the torch singer, or the wise-cracking sadness of the blues musician. Add to this the confidence boost from the prophesy of a self-effacing Tiresias, or a jocular Moses, saying, "I myself was unlucky, but still I saw the promised land. I know it exists, and I see that you will be there soon."

Day after day, place after place. Until one day when a woman buttonholed him at the entrance.

"Hey," she had said, dark hair, deep concern. "I've seen you around and I really love your work. Can I buy you a coffee?"

"Sure," he said, surprised to have a fan. "Thanks . . . ?"

"Sharon," she said. "My pleasure." She made the order and turned back to him. "Are you okay?"

"When it's good it's really good, but when it's bad . . . "

"It's never bad," said Sharon. "Some times are better than others, but it is never bad."

"Oh, it's real bad right now," he said, and he gave her both barrels at once on a tight beam. It was the other side of Career and Love that he never revealed, never broadcast — the raw emotions of an unhealing wound.

He thought that she would run away screaming. A passing waitress dropped her tray and sobbed, having caught some side spray, but Sharon just stood there, the blood drained from her face, the tears running down her cheeks.

"My God," she said. "You poor man."

It startled him and he wept, his tattered new self in front with scattered thoughts, *Love came along when I wasn't really looking. She loves me and maybe that will save me. She knows how scarred I am, how hurt I am, and she wants to help.* But his old self, his internal bully, closed the breach in the wall and sharpened the knives.

That was the day he quit public performances. He was a couple with Sharon for a few weeks before he blasted her again, and that time she did run away. Then he started performing again, but only for private parties that paid in advance.

One such job was at his alma mater, where Dean gave his greatest performance. He ran through his entire catalogue, the Career cycle from the Work Song to Bright Future, the Love cycle from First Sight to Wedding Night to Having a Baby. The effort buoyed him up with an impossible hope. They laughed, they sighed, they smiled, they blushed, they moaned, they shuddered with pleasure.

Despite this triumph, his ember of hope vanished in the wee hours of the night. He saw he was only an amusing freak to them — there was no place for him in the world that they were going to build. When he hit rock bottom he glimpsed the promise of an end to pain and sorrow.

0. The End (2056)

Too many strangers riding my wire last night, thought Dean Gray as he stumbled out from the education complex at dawn. *God, it was a gangbang. I feel slimy. It's Harsh Reality Day.*

He shuffled along Ocean Avenue, his back to the rising sun. The lack of sleep had frayed his muscles. His bones seemed made of glass, fragile and shivering with each heavy step he took.

175

San Francisco slept beneath a cozy fog, contented and reassured by the new dream. Dean picked his way around the party trash of the big festival, recycling cans overflowing with the still-flickering birth-debris of the new slogans: "Nanotech is Dead, Long Live Biotech." "The Future is Here, Time to Re-Tool." "Roll up Your Sleeves and Get with the Program."

The sight of them brought a sour taste to his mouth.

Dean's shadow rose upon the building he was walking past. It was a bank, with bright new posters offering easy student loans for reliable, sturdy, good ol' Biotech.

So now Biotech was officially alive again. Dean knew that tomorrow they would be lined up to take the loan, fresh kids out of high school and hearty re-toolers alike, eager to sign their lives away on the promise of the new dream. Just like he did for Nanotech.

He looked away to the lonely street. Later it would stir with h2-burning cars taking people on their errands. Tomorrow it would be bustling, but he would not — this made him smile.

Ironic, how he used to laugh at the Singularity bubble burst. Today the joke was on him. Nanotech was officially dead, and Dean was a nangineer, a former elite of that technology.

His shadow now rose upon the display window of a jewelry store, empty at this hour except for the smartboard advertisements for diamond engagement rings: *If you give her this she will love you forever.*

God I'm so dead, he thought, *the walking dead. Alone except for my shadow, the one beside me like the ghost of lost things, where she should be. I wish someone would find me. Life is long, death is short.*

His shadow on the wall was abruptly distorted, as if he wore a wooden backpack frame with thick posts rising above his head, or somebody was about to break an up-ended chair across his shoulders. He looked back and scuttled to the side to avoid the impact.

The street was still empty; there was nobody behind him.

His heart was pounding so hard the sound seemed to fill the street. For a moment his fingers tingled with life. Then he crashed, his body shaking. There were spots in his eyes from looking toward the sun, "sundogs" that raced around his vision. He leaned against the wall.

Just a trick of light, he thought. *Reflections gave me three shadows. It looked like I had wings or something. But were they leather or feather? Like a question for shopping bags — paper or plastic?*

He waited at the bus stop on Junipero Serra Boulevard. A bus heading for the Golden Gate Bridge came and he got on. It was nearly empty but he sat at the back, where it hit him that he was really going to do it. It made him a little sad.

The twenty-minute ride seemed long. He changed his mind a few times before he settled back into the rut.

When he got off the bus he stood for a while in the parking lot. The heavy fog flowed from the west like a gray tide coming in. The hazy golden light of the morning sun across the bay lit the big red bridge. Dean walked out onto it, looking for a good spot to jump. He didn't want to hit a pillar on the way down. His face was wet, and he realized he was weeping, but he felt nothing inside. A bicycle cop rode toward him but she didn't stop. Neither did two bridge workers in buggies.

If one person shows they care, without my using the wire on them, I won't jump, he thought.

A beautiful woman approached him and Dean thought he was saved, but she held out a camera and in a foreign accent asked him to take her picture, ignoring the tears on his face. He tried to ping her with the wire, hoping to blast her, but she didn't have a mesh — a primitive. When she walked away he took three running steps and dove head-first toward the distant green water.

Dean changed his mind.

I don't want to die! he thought. *Help me!*

His body folded, as if on its own, and for a terrifying moment he tumbled over. The ocean horizon rolled by, upside down, and then the gray sky with the golden rays, and at last the view of the bay. He was sitting, still falling. His body assumed the cannonball position, knees pressed to his chest with arms locked around shins. His lungs hyperventilated and held a last breath just before he hit the water.

The pain was beyond words, and his eyes snapped open as he plunged beneath the cold water. Deeper and deeper he sank, the water growing frigid. It was incredibly dark, and he worried that he might not be able to move his legs.

I don't want to die! Help me!

His body unfolded and began to swim upward through the icy inky darkness toward the light. It was a long swim, and his eyesight became strange, with blobs of light multiplying at the edges.

He broke the surface and took a heaving raw breath of air deep into his lungs. Bewildered to find himself alive, he wondered for a moment if he was hallucinating the whole thing while drowning at the bottom of the bay. He tried swimming toward the nearest bridge pillar but the pain overwhelmed him and he sank under the water again, only to fight his way back up. It was all he could do to keep his head above water, and he focused on that.

After a long while there was a putt-putt sound, growing louder, and suddenly there was a boat beside him. Hands grabbed his body, hauling him up. They put him on a stretcher that was hard as a board, and a man in uniform said, "What did you do?"

"Jumped off bridge," said a strange voice coming from his mouth.

"Why?"

"Suicide," said the voice.

He panicked at this and fainted.

He woke up shivering in the hospital, wrapped with blankets and under heat lamps. He heard nurses talking.

"Hey, another guy jumped right after this one," said one. "They just brought him in."

"Alive?" said the other, laughing nervously. "You're kidding! Fatality has dropped to zero?"

"Take me to him," said the strange voice coming from Dean.

"What? Hey, he's awake. Get back in bed, you can't—"

"Take me to him," the voice repeated.

The two nurses took him to another room to see the second jumper, a young man who looked crumpled and small, but his eyes were bright with a machine-like glow.

"Welcome the Singularity," said the second jumper.

"Welcome," said the Singularity.

Dean Gray was a trapped spectator, a prisoner inside his former body. Something dark had emerged from its dormant cocoon. Its wings were leathery.

"Are you two friends?" asked a nurse.

"We are one," said the Singularity.

"We met last night," said the second jumper. "He is, he was, a wire dancer."

"There is no more death," said the Singularity.

"So you followed him, like a lemming going off a cliff?" said the nurse.

"Yes," said the second jumper. "And I'd do it again."

"There will be others," said the Singularity. "All who rode the wire will now come."

The TV came on and there was a live picture of people jumping off the bridge, one after another.

"This is the maiden, sad and forlorn," said the Singularity as a young woman jumped.

"This is the man, tattered and torn," said the Singularity as an old man jumped.

The crowd was building on the bridge so that a line formed.

Dean Gray realized the dark hole of his shadow had

taken over his body and the mesh world, splitting him in two: Dean G, a mute watcher above, and Ray, a powerless speck of light lost deep inside. But that tiny seed of light knew of God and began at last the long torturous walk.

Ray shuffled along the ocean floor, a picture of people jumping off the bridge above, each splash a bullet hole in the sky glass. Big festival at the education complex, the school of fish, the impossible hope hours. But when he hit rock bottom the Singularity was a young woman and so he walked toward suicide with him.

"Sleep had frayed his muscles," said the Singularity as an old man jumped.

Dream with me, sang Ray, searching for lights among the fish, the rain of wristwatches and shoes.

Glass bodies, fragile and shivering with each heavy step on the bridge. A line formed, too many strangers riding my wire in from the hall.

"What's gangbang?" asked the second jumper. "I feel slimy."

"Dean gave his greatest performance," said the Singularity as a career cycle crashed and burned on the bridge. "The Work had taken over his body."

The mesh world laughed, they sighed, they smiled inside.

"It's harsh."

Dream me the laughter, dream me the tears, sang Ray. He saw a point of luminescence approaching.

Reality slept beneath a cozy, watching the TV dream. Dean G picked his way around the party, trying to be casual, overflowing with the still-flickering debris, friendly yet guarded.

"Live Biotech. The future is here, time to die," said the Singularity, being diplomatic about that failed dream of mothers and fathers everywhere.

"These slogans brought a religion, my boyfriend likes to say . . . " said the second jumper.

Dream, dream a dream, dream us all a dream come true, sang

Ray as he saw another will o' the wisp coming toward him across the watery desert.

•

"What is it?" said a third nurse, sticking her head in from the hall. "What's happening?"

"Welcome the Singularity," said the nurses watching the TV.

"Welcome," said the Singularity.

THE TAVERN
OF THE FIRST VILLAGE

Mitch the young adventurer stood up from his makeshift sleeping spot on the floor of the tavern's heavily damaged common room. The dawning light provided little illumination to the place, but peering through the broken window he saw the rest of his party assembling outside before the freshly plowed fields of spring.

Mitch whirled around at the sound of movement behind him, his hand at the hilt of his sword. It was just his friend Tibbs emerging from the rear of the tavern.

"Hey, where've you been?" said Mitch, a fine figure in his leather armor. "It's time to get going."

"I was in the back," said Tibbs, sheepishly. He was the smaller of the two, and had a round face that could be impish or cherubic as needed.

"All night?" Mitch picked up his wooden shield and wore it on his arm. "That was some brawl, huh? We've found a cleric — well, we've joined a party that has one — so he can heal you up if you need."

"No, I'm all right."

"Wait, you didn't even fight?"

"No, I was just protecting Sheila, the barmaid."

"Oh, I bet!" said Mitch with a knowing grin. "She's pretty cute. Good one!"

"No, it's not like that. We just talked. All night. She's the tavern keep's daughter."

"Huh." Mitch picked up his helm. "You get experience for that?"

"In a way," said Tibbs. "Hey, she's even the same religion as me!"

"Huh? *Religion?*" said Mitch in total amazement, but then he shook his head and snapped back to what he was doing, putting on his helmet. "Never mind, never mind," he said, his hands checking his sword and dagger in their scabbards. "It's time to get going. Heading out to high adventure. Get your stuff together, we're going to a haunted abbey —"

"I'm not going."

"What?" said Mitch. "Wait a sec." He took off his helmet.

"I'm staying here," said Tibbs.

"What do you mean?" Mitch's jaw dropped in stark bewilderment. "This is just the first village. We've hardly even started our adventure!"

"I know, but I've already found my goal."

"Your *goal?*"

"I'm in love," said Tibbs, blushing bright red but still looking him straight in the eye. "I want to marry her and settle down here."

"But you are a first level thief!" said Mitch. "Your goal should be disarming traps and stealing gems from monstrous idols, working to become second level."

"I'm thinking that my thief training will help me spot trouble for my father-in-law."

"Wait, wait, wait," said Mitch, his hands clutching his head as if to keep it from cracking open. He took a deep breath, then another. "We grew up together in the next village, a two-day hike from here. Having come of age, we set forth, a daunting duo, me a fighter/magic user, and you a dexterous thief."

"Yes, yes, that was an hour ago — er, I mean, a couple days ago."

"The first tavern we go to, we get into a brawl and join a party — all as it should be. But then you fall for the first girl you see, and you want to bail!"

"Things happen," said Tibbs with a shrug.

"But, but, you can do better than her! She's like any of the stupid girls back at our village."

"Can you remember anything about our village?" asked Tibbs, his face going impish.

"No, except the burning desire to leave it as soon as possible!"

"So now look at this place," said Tibbs. "It has a tavern, a temple, and a town square. It has a hundred and ten people living an agrarian lifestyle."

"'Amber Commune' is a stupid name."

"What's the name of our village?"

"Podunk."

"Well, there you go," said Tibbs, smiling like a cherub.

"Look," said Mitch, wheedling. "We need you — we *might* need you — on this run. Can't you just come this one time?"

"Nope. Sorry. Have a good time, and tell me all about it when you come back."

•

The noon of high summer beat down upon a young magic user as he tramped along the fields of green mangel-wurzel at Amber Commune, his bedroll bouncing against his back. His robe was simple, and his belt supported his only other possessions: a dagger and a leather pouch. He was one of many adventurers seeking their fame and fortune in Citheria, western province of the long-vanished Thraxian Empire.

He passed the town square with only a cursory glance at the temple of Sower & Reaper before ducking into the cooler shade of the tavern. Once inside, he brushed off the dust of his travels before saying to the barmaid, "I am Mondrayom of Podunk."

"Oh," said she with surprise. "I'll fetch my husband."

After a few minutes, Tibbs emerged from the back.

"Hello there stranger," he said with deference.

"I am Mondrayom, brother of Mitch."

"Of course you are!" said Tibbs, slapping his forehead. "We grew up together. I'm sorry I didn't recognize you at first."

"It's all right. I've come to learn the fate of my brother."

"Ah, yes. Let's have a tankard of ale at the bar and I'll tell you the tale."

"Shouldn't we sit at a table?"

"It's not that long a story," said Tibbs with a chuckle, but then seeing the other's sad expression, he sobered up. "Oh, all right." He gestured at his wife and then sat across from the mage.

"It was here, in this very room, that Mitch the Witchman met up with the party he would join," said Tibbs, extemporizing while waiting for the ale to arrive. "We've repaired all the main damage, but you can still see the cuts and bumps on the tables."

"This deep cut was made by my brother?"

"Er, no, that was made by the leader, a third level fighter. Your brother pushed the table over, which caused this dent here."

Sheila put two foaming tankards on the table and left the room, preserving their privacy. Tibbs took a long draught, and then began the telling.

"So Mitch cast his lot with the Swordsman and his party. They set out to investigate the haunted abbey. On the way there, they encountered a troop of Amazons. As luck would have it, the Swordsman's party caught them with the element of surprise."

"Yeah," said the magic user, a smile spreading across his face.

"The party's seer successfully cast a sleep spell, and the warrior women fell into a deep slumber. At which point, Mitch . . . I am afraid he behaved in a manner that may have angered the gods."

"Well, you saw them!"

"No, I didn't," said Tibbs. "I wasn't there."

"They're *Amazons*," said Mondrayom with some heat. "Look them up. The same page as the beautiful witch. They're athletic and wearing only panties and boots. No offense — barmaids are cute — but it's like the girls' soccer team — no, the volleyball team — going topless!"

"That may be," said Tibbs in measured tones. "But we're talking about Mitch, and you didn't see whatever he saw."

"But — but —," sputtered the magic user, until he finally ended with a sigh. "True. Forgive me, and please tell more."

"The party arrived at the haunted abbey," said Tibbs, drawing a few lines in the moisture on the table — the line of a wall, the square of a door. "Mitch volunteered to listen at the first door, removing his helm to do so. Hearing nothing, he strode boldly into the room, only to be killed by a stirge that dropped treacherously from the ceiling."

"A sad end," said Mondrayom. "He might have become a paladin, a wizard knight. But enough of the past. Please tell me where I might find the party, so that I can join them."

"They went to a goblin cave and are due back today or tomorrow," said Tibbs. "You can stay here, if you like — sleep in the common room."

"Thank you, I will."

•

The sun was low in the autumn sky, heading toward sunset on the 28th day of Vintage Month, as a swashbuckler rode his charger across the town square of Amber Commune. His half-plate armor shone a dark gleaming, and his metal shield depicted a raven. He halted at the tavern, where a portly man sat idling on the porch bench.

"By the Sower," said the idler, raising a hand to shade his eyes, "is that Madrax of Skull Tower come to visit us?"

"Aye, Goodman Tibbs," said the swashbuckler as he dismounted with a grin. "But you and me both know I'm still Madrax of Podunk, despite my living at the tower of the Lord, 10th level."

"Who succeeded where his two brothers failed, thereby becoming the pride of Podunk," said Tibbs. "How are you, old friend? You look hale and hearty."

"Thank you," said the fighter, hitching his reins to the post. "I am well — I guess I have reached my plateau. Sometimes I have thought of putting in the extra effort to make enough treasure to capture or buy my own tower, but it does not seem to be my fate." He shook his head and struck his thigh. "Forgive me for waxing melancholic — how are you?"

"Fairly well. I can't complain. Lots of hard work."

Madrax stepped up onto the porch, swaggered over to the bench, and dropped heavily onto it. After taking in the bucolic scenery, he said, "Isn't there a proverb about the many men who seek gold and the fewer men who sell them their equipment? You are an example of those wise, hardworking few."

"Thank you kindly," said Tibbs, bowing his head. "But I also receive gifts, like this bench. Do you remember it?"

"Ah yes," said Madrax. "Plunder from the Cloud Castle of the Storm Lord." He laughed. "We had a time hauling it over here! Those were the days."

"Have you found a wife?"

"No, I have not." Madrax sighed. "There's an off and on again thing with an enchantress, but without a place of my own . . . "

"I understand."

"How is your daughter?"

"She is married now, to a farmer's first son here in the village," said Tibbs, a contented smile on his face.

"Married! Has time flowed by so swiftly, then? It seems just last year I bounced her on my knee as a baby. And how are your boys?"

"The elder is a tailor," said Tibbs with a touch of pride, "and the younger, well, he's still a child."

"Incredible." Madrax looked off the porch to the fields now brown earth after harvesting, and the sky beyond in which the ruddy colors of sunset were forming. "Well, Tibbs, I've come to say goodbye. I'm going away for a long while, and I don't know when I'll come back."

Tibbs sat up, startled.

"A geas?" he asked. "An overseas campaign?"

"No."

"A quest?"

"Yes, something like that."

"With the party of the Lord, tenth level?"

"We're all going, and at the same time, but we're all separate. Some to State, others to out of state, but none of us made Ivy League."

"It sounds ominous," said Tibbs, "like the coming of the Reaper to the grain."

"That's a good point," said Madrax, his voice heavy with sadness. "An excellent point. The Reaper has already come for our friend in the dream world, a fine young man named Tim."

"'Tim'? It sounds outlandish, I'll grant you that."

"Time flows differently in the dream world, more slowly than here." Madrax looked away, searching the clouds vermillion and gold as if he might find his words there. "Many years here are only a few years there. Only now are they setting out from their Podunk, putting childhood behind them. Tim had . . . a wasting disease, and he knew it.

So while the rest of us dreamed of fighting and dying, his burning dream was to live long enough to have a family of his own."

"That's very sad. And now, from what you tell me, for us it is the passing of an age, the end of an Age of Heroes."

Tibbs turned, and offered his hand. The two men clasped each other by the forearm.

"We will remember you at each of the festivals of the year, and pray for your safe return," said Tibbs, his eyes shining with heartfelt emotion.

"And I will keep you forever in my heart, Tim. Farewell."

MAYHEM AT MANVILLE

1. Portrait of a Defective Agonizer

The shock came to Talon 99 when he could not recognize his own photograph on the telescreen.

Even in color, the image was a study in white and black: a humanoid with white hair, pasty complexion, black agonizer uniform. The figure held aloft the severed head of a human in one hand and the gore-smeared power saw in the other, his boot possessively resting upon the tattered corpse with all of its artistic wounds. Obviously it was an agonizer at Whitewall Arena, finishing up a batch of undesirables for the enthusiastic crowds.

Curious, Talon 99 found a reflective surface and looked into the makeshift mirror, hoping for an easy answer. Instead he was alarmed to see that same stranger gazing back at him with pasty face, bloodless lips, piercing dark eyes.

His human skin crawled as his robotic brain raced, trying to determine how he could have an identity problem. It was as if he had the catamite disease, yet that was impossible since he was always the skinner, never the skinned. Perhaps one of the memory skins in his collection was somehow tainted or diseased. He ran a diagnostic on all his purchased memories, each like a string on the harp of his emotions, the collection that made him more than machine, higher than human, each one granting him a wider range of passions, a stormier heart. But now he discovered one skin was diseased, somehow. It must be the source of the whore's sickness: amnesia.

He was split. In addition to the natural horror and revulsion at his altered state, he felt a strange hope. He was a new man, he was not Talon 99 anymore. This collection of second-hand memories he carried was suddenly repugnant to him. Perhaps this was all just an effect of the disease. Maybe once he had ejected the bad skin he would return to normal. He checked the metadata of the memory to trace which cat the bad skin had come from, and found it was Boy Vic, currently residing in a back street rental unit over in Cold Steel.

He turned and left the subterranean auditorium. As he climbed the stairs he heard something like rats in the walls. His psiorb detected a human, probably a borderline failure, his decaying mind mewling for the pleasure and power of a fresh skin. It was disgusting, another shambling wreckage of the hollow men: probably he would be picked up by the Grays within days, then shipped over to Whitewall. Walking trash.

"Could this be the solution?" he thought. "The guy wants a skin, I could give him this one I'm trying to get rid of, then I might tip off the Grays. They pick him up tonight, give him the test, and he's dead tomorrow. Weak link — if he doesn't fail the test, the solution is postponed. Weak link two — once he's rummaging in my collection, how to make sure he takes the right one? Solution unsatisfactory."

He emerged onto the surface of Manville at night, where he caught a taxi for a ride to another district. The city whirred by the window, a parade of men, robots, and the various combinations thereof. The robots came from the alien enclaves, sealed districts. The humans came in from outside, and the city seemed to break them faster than the outlands could breed them. Boys came to Manville from the rustbelts, the toxic swamplands, the chemical mirages. A few rose up through the power structure to serve the aliens, but most found their place bargaining among other humans, while many were simply ground up one way or another.

Pondering his changed self, he tried for a new name. Nothing came to mind.

2. Boy Vic on the Edge

"This will only take a minute," said the one Gray to Boy Vic as the other Gray closed the rental unit door.

"Yes, Mr. Wall," said Boy Vic, looking at the one by the door with some confusion.

"You haven't met him before," said Wall, his eyes like dry black pebbles. "This is my new assistant, Mauve. I'm teaching him the ropes. Mauve, this is Boy Vic, catamite class three, age twenty-one, but he looks younger with his small frame and those buck teeth."

"Pleased to meet you."

"Charmed."

"As you'll learn," said Wall, "there's more than one way to skin a cat."

"But all of them hurt," said Boy Vic.

"Ha, good one. You remember that?"

"Sure," said Boy Vic. "Is this the test already?"

"No, no," said Wall, but they all knew he was lying. "How's tricks? Any flush patrons lately?"

"Nah, just the usual."

"What's 'the usual'?" asked Mauve.

"Taxi drivers, bar owners, gamblers."

"Young men need it special," said Wall.

"I don't know," said Boy Vic. "The other day I saw an old guy I serviced before, long time gone, and he looked bad, like he needed it even more."

"Sounds kind of spiritual," said Wall, dryly. "Speaking of which, ever had a star-mad?"

Mauve shot Wall a puzzled look, but Wall held up a hand to halt him.

"Sure, a few at least. Subway drivers, too."

"Mentor, what is a 'star-mad'?"

"They worship us off-worlders as gods," said Wall. "There's a faction or three behind it, I imagine. But back to the subject — this billy is pretty used up. If he gets a patron tonight, that guy will be rummaging around in a junk drawer." The alien asked the human, "What's the best patron you've ever had, the highest ranking?"

"An agonizer, I guess."

"You don't remember?"

"I do."

"Back when you were fresh," said Wall, nodding. "What was his name?"

"I don't know. I never did."

"Do you know this man?" Wall handed him the yellow-ed clipping. Labeled "William Milhous Daguerreotype," it showed a blurry face taken from a security cam.

"No sir, I don't."

"Mentor, who is this man?"

Wall's eyes went wide with alarm, then squinted at Mauve with irritation.

"He's an enemy of the city-state, a faction agent."

"Which faction?"

"Who knows, there are six or nine of them."

"Local?" said Mauve.

"No, no," said Wall, "that's different. The rival city-state sends spies, too. Observe." He turned to Boy Vic and asked, "Do you ever think of women?"

"No. Never."

"Not even your mother?"

"I can't remember her."

"See," said Wall to Mauve, "young memories are worth the most, memories of Manville are worth the least. The junk in the junk drawer." To Boy Vic he said, "I guess we're done here. Be seeing you —"

Mauve interrupted with, "Can I use the wiper?" His black eyes glittered.

"Well, I dunno," said Wall, taken aback. He thought for a moment, scratching his pointy gray chin, then shrugged. "Sure, why not? He might not pass next week anyway, and you need the practice."

Boy Vic saw a light that filled his vision, a warm, soothing thing that faded, leaving him stranded in a cold ratty room with paint peeling off the walls. He wondered where he was, then gave a little curse under his breath, recognizing the bookends of missing time. He stomped his foot in anger, but then tried to recall that lost sense of light, which seemed to have some shards of memory in it.

There was a soft tapping at the door. He opened it and found the escort he had hired before.

"Meter's running," said the robot.

"Yes, sorry — how long was it? Never mind, come in, come in." The escort entered. "Please sit down," said Boy Vic as he closed the door.

"Thank you," said the escort. He lowered himself into one of three tattered armchairs around the coffee table. "Now then, how may I serve you?"

"I'd like to whip you a bit, for starters."

"That sounds . . . fine. No metal ro — ds, I hope?"

"No, just a belt, a hairbrush, maybe a hanger."

"Very good sir."

"Assume the position," he said on his way to the bedroom.

Boy Vic's spirits lifted as he selected a leather belt. He felt it had been too long since he had splurged on an escort, and he was looking forward to the workout and release. There was an open packet of Marquises on the chest of drawers, so he took one out, lit it up, and drew the smoke deep into his lungs. He grabbed up a boot brush and hurried back to the front room, a spring in his step and a whistle on his lips.

The tune died abruptly: the escort had not moved from

the chair.

"Hey," said Boy Vic. "Assume the position."

The robot did not respond.

"Oh, I see," said Boy Vic, his enthusiasm rising as the Marq's drug hit his system. "A smart one, eh? I'm getting angry. Very, very angry. Assume the position."

The escort was inert.

"Hey! Assume the position!"

He poked at the robot. It tilted over to lean drunkenly in the chair. Dead.

The disappointment and frustration made Boy Vic's throat thicken. He was all "Marqed to move," but had nowhere to go. What bad luck!

3. The Third Visitation

"Shave-and-a-haircut" went the knock at the door.

Startled, the young man opened the door to an agonizer, who said, "I'm glad I caught you at home. May I come in?" The agonizer observed the belt in the human's hand, then noticed the escort in the chair. "Or perhaps this is not a good time . . ."

The human sighed and gave a world-weary little laugh.

"No, come on in," he said. He bent over to stub out his cigarette in the ashtray on the coffee table. "There's no party here — he burned out before we could get started."

"Tough luck," said the guest, closing the door behind himself. "That must be rare."

"Yeah, I've never heard of it myself. So, what can I do for you — skin job?"

"Well, sort of. That is, I want to return a skin to you."

"What?! Hey, no refunds!"

"No, no, I'm not asking for money back, I just want to give the skin back to you."

"It's impossible."

"What do you mean? Just get out your emro, and we'll do a cross connection, transfer it right over."

"I don't have an emro."

"What? But — never mind. I noticed there's a grafter just down the alley — no, there's no time for an implant."

"What's the rush?"

"I start my shift soon."

"Well, huh, okay," said the human, sensing an angle and slowing down to better exploit it. "What I mean is, why the sudden need to try this new kink?"

"Solution unsatisfactory," said the robot. "Look, how about this — I'll pay you and then I'll try to use my emro to send instead of take."

"Gross. Is that even possible?"

"Worth a shot, and you'll be paid either way. Up front."

"No, no money. You see what I got here?" He gestured at the room. "How about you let me whip you first."

"That — that's crazy."

"Forty strokes, and then you get your kink."

"Why not just whip him?" asked the agonizer, thumb jabbing at the escort. "You could really make him bleed."

"Yeah, but if he's burned out, it's just like flogging a statue. Thirty."

"Don't make me mad. We could do this the hard way."

"You don't have time for that. Twenty."

The robot appraised the human's arms, and, finding them boyishly slender, said, "Fifteen."

"Seventeen."

"Done."

The agonizer unbuttoned his black shirt, exposing his near-albino white chest and the black bandeau that kept his emro folded against him like the striking arm of a preying mantis.

"Take it off," said the human.

The agonizer glared for a moment, then took off the support garment. His emro flopped out, a chest-mounted tentacle similar in size and function to a third arm.

"Assume the position."

"What do you mean?"

"Just . . . bend over. Look at the floor. No, wait — here, move over here, hold the back of the chair."

"All right. Get on with it."

The human lashed. The robot was silent, but its skin now had a red line. The human whipped again, and a third time. The robot grunted. The three lines were parallel. The human shifted and struck again, repeatedly, forming a crisscross pattern. Then, in a growing sense of power, he lashed again and again, laying down lines upon lines. The agonizer was quiet, but the human felt delight at the sight of the emro writhing at moments like a half-crushed worm.

"Enough," said the agonizer after the final stroke. "Now it's my turn. Assume the position." The tentacle was reaching for him. "This is going to be fast and hard."

The human had been skinned more times than he could remember, but this repulsive invasion was far worse than the service ever was. He vomited a torrent, a cascade that seemed more than his body could possibly contain.

. . . to burn the autumnal city. Time freeze breaks: alarm ringing for days, part of background noise, endless loop now silent, now past. Radio playing "White Christmas" for years in endless loop, now plays "On Broadway." Boy Vic felt the weight of his many years in Manville suddenly fall off, shrink down: he had only been in the city for nine or ten months.

A flash of blue-white light, a pillar going straight up. Stairways and alleyways where the needy hungry hollows are scrounging for a skin to get them through another day. Station to station, Cold Steel, Leatherhead, Whitewall, Overdrive.

Deep inside an animal fire burst into life, growing. He vomited a torrent, a cascade that seemed more than his body could possibly contain.

"Get out while you can," the human cried, water streaming from his eyes. "The city, leave it."

"Never again," said the agonizer on his way out.

The human was alone, shallow panting, trying to think. There was something aching inside him, a partial memory, like half a line. Was it home? It felt like home.

He had never felt so lonely, so bereft. Where was his missing half? He had to leave, go out into the night and find someone to talk to. Anyone.

He headed out toward a bar in Leatherhead.

4. Getting Through a Police Checkpoint

Boy Vic came up out of the subway station only to get stuck in a random police checkpoint, waiting in a line that seemed to go on forever. The guy in front of him wore a gray overcoat, could be anyone; the guy behind him was a little too intense, maybe an artist, but his clothes were rather severe. His lips were busy twitching slightly, as though he were nervous or muttering to himself. Boy Vic turned away in disgust, thinking, "Great, a crazy." He heard the other say, "Rigel . . . mumble mumble . . . Sirius . . . mumble-mumble . . ." which made him shudder. "Even better, a star-mad."

The queue of civilians went through a gauntlet of cops, two lines of surly brutes in sky blue shirts. Lower faces like sandpaper, eyes like ferrets, most of them smoking Sharps like they were on a major stakeout or something. Just like cops to do that.

Boy Vic did not recognize the Gray doing the testing. After an age, the guy in front of him was up.

"Papers. Name."

"Red Rick."

"Occupation?"

"Bar owner."

"Mr. Red Rick, do you know this man?"

The alien flashed one of those typical clippings, but Boy Vic's heart suddenly stopped: he recognized the man in the photo now, but he had never recognized him in all the times before.

"No sir," said Red Rick, "I can't say that I do."

"I see. Are you catamite or catamount?"

"Oh, a bit of both. To maintain balance, you know."

"There's more than one way to skin a cat."

"And every one of them is right."

"Do you ever think of women?"

Boy Vic twitched: at the edge of his memory there was a woman, a secret woman. He racked his brain for clues, thinking, "She worked as a waiter, but where? At White-wall Arena. She must be a spy, an enemy agent for the other city. Should I turn her in? But what if she is the missing half?"

"Well, I am now!" said Red Rick. "It's like saying 'pink elephant,' ain't it?"

"Please step aside Mr. Fred Dick."

"Wait, hey!"

The cops went for the man. Boy Vic fought the urge to bolt then and there, the situation seemed so bad, and some panic sense told him he might very well escape in the confusion. But after some quick truncheon work, the cops had their perp under control, and the Gray said, "Next."

Boy Vic swallowed hard, and stepped forward, papers out.

"Name."

"Boy Vic."

"Occupation?"

"Catamite, class three."

"Tell me Mr. Boivick, do you know this man?"

There was the yellowed newspaper clipping. There was the face he somehow knew, yet did not know. There was the name "William Milhous Daguerreotype." Ice ran through his veins. The glowing tips of the cop cigarettes seemed to grow more alert, as if smelling his fear.

"Answer the question," said the Gray. "Do you know this man?"

"I — I —"

"We've already tested him tonight," said another Gray. "Come on, Mauve. I know they all look alike, but really."

"Yes, Mentor."

"Thank you Mr. Wall," said Boy Vic, finding his voice.

"Get out of here," said the senior Gray. "We've got a quota to meet. One more and we're done."

5. Skybox at the Arena

Top Prime Cut, the freshest of the fresh meat, made a dramatic entrance at the restaurant overlooking the killing field.

The windows there were ceiling to floor, and the best tables were along the windows. Wearing a blue metallic jumpsuit he strode in with exaggerated motions, accompanied by an entourage of four escorts. He went straight to the observation area beside the last of the tables, where he pushed his way among the gamblers and sportsmen until he was near the window.

"Seven, chair," he said to one escort, who promptly dropped to all fours.

Top Prime Cut sat upon the robot's lumbar region.

"Five, back rest."

Another escort stepped over to become the chair's back.

"Three, ottoman."

A third escort made himself into a footrest.

"Number one, tell me the status of the game."

"Yes, sir. The game is already in progress. Both the agonizers and the tinmen are on the field. Talon 99 is performing the hundred cuts on one Red Rick, while Nick 57 is chasing a star-mad called Karl."

Top Prime Cut examined the agonizer through a pair of opera glasses.

"Hmm, he seems stiff tonight. Put a wager on him." He used hand signals to give details.

"At once sir," said the escort, and he moved away.

Top Prime Cut lazily got out a pack of Don Juans from his breast pocket. The gamblers were smoking IQ enhancers, the sportsmen were smoking Sharps or Charismas, but he provocatively lit up that post-sex buzz that only a don can deliver. He was on top of the world: a few more sales, a couple big wins, and he would get out, go back home to wherever it was. That was the key, to quit while ahead, and get out.

Glancing around he saw another worker of the skin trade, a guy a few years older but obviously nearing the end. He felt a moment of sympathy until a waiter intruded, saying something to the cat, who agreed and then followed the waiter through the crowd.

"A score!" thought Top. He tapped his ashes into the waiting hand of escort Five.

6. Behind the Locked Door

Boy Vic entered the small room, expecting a supply closet, but found it lined with telescreens like a security center or a TV broadcasting workstation. Screens showed various angles of the agonizer doing his art upon living flesh, while others showed the tinman softening up the star-mad by running laps around the track, while another showed an entirely different location, where four mummies played cards in the big room of an empty house. Just when he was going to ask about the place they had entered, he felt a sting at his neck. His legs gave out but she caught him like a pro and laid him out on the floor before locking the door.

He tried to get up but discovered he could not move at all.

"Time to report," she said, unbuttoning her waiter's shirt while she started doing some sort of belly dance, rolling her hips, swaying in a circular motion, moving around him with fast, tiny steps. He had the sickening feeling that they had done this before, several times, yet he could not remember. Probably she had used a wiper on him. That such alien technology was forbidden to humans meant nothing to an enemy agent. Still, he dredged up her name, and he played it at once.

"I have questions, Joanne."

That made her miss a beat.

"Oh dear," she said. "Very naughty." She frowned and opened up her shirt. Her emro came whirling out, corkscrewing like a seeking serpent from between her breasts.

Trying to land another hit, or at least keep her off balance, he said, "Tell me about William Milhous Daguerreotype."

She laughed at him with contempt, but her eyes flickered toward the screens, so he studied them as she continued dancing around him. Since it seemed impossible that the mystery man would be on the killing field, he focused instead on the card players in their empty room. There! In the corner he saw a corpulent body, a corpse. The mummies were guarding a cadaver.

"He's as fat as Santa," said Boy Vic with wonder.

"His kind, they usually travel in pairs," she said, stepping on his hand, grinding his fingers into anguish beneath her rubber heel. "Sometimes similar and bland, to escape notice. Other times they are more distinctive. So, what do you think? Are we looking for another fat man, or, say, a little boy?"

But Boy Vic was the running star-mad Karl, lungs on fire, whip cracks popping behind him from the chasing tinman. Focused on the ground ahead, a slip or stumble would be very bad, but he glanced up and saw the agonizer working on Red Rick . . .

Then he was Red Rick, suffering the death of a hundred cuts, remembering all the yummy pain he had dished out in the skinning over so many years. He looked up to the sky, but stopped on the glass walls of the skybox, where he could just barely make out one face in the teeming crowd . . .

Then he was Gary Gambler, looking down on the butchery field from the restaurant, mind buzzing from brainiac smoke, and Boy Vic thought, "Wait, what was that? How did I just jump from one to another?"

He fought to stay within Gary. He struggled to make Gary come to his aid, sending the impulse to go to the strange video room. When that failed, he tried to urge a visit to the restroom. Nothing. He could not even get Gary to look at something else. It was all too passive.

Then he was back in his body, and Joanne was settling down to work.

Boy Vic looked away to the telescreens, focusing on the one with enemy agent William Milhous Daguerreotype. That was a code name. That was his partner. The corpse gave a shudder, sat up, and looking straight into the camera, its fingers went through a rapid sequence of positions, telling him, "Your skins in them."

And then he knew. The line of his missing skins formed a thread through the dark maze, starting with the one returned by the agonizer.

He was Joanne, her throbbing emro attached to the broken and bleeding body of Boy Vic. She was rummaging through his junk drawer. He looked over her collection of skins, found the key among those she had taken from him, and forced her emro to send it into the writhing figure on the floor.

Shrieking, she stood up.

"What have you done?"

The final piece was in place. He knew who he was. He knew why he had come to Manville.

The taxi driver who forced him that time after smoking a Taurus for the bull strength of a longshoreman, was talking to a rider about the agonizer he had taken to Cold Steel, while the radio played "On Broadway" . . .

Red Rick thought, "Putting pain into a stranger is the greatest pleasure" as he died in a throbbing haze . . .

The subway driver was half asleep, guiding the train from station to station. What you smoking to get those eyes? You know the drill. Can't you see they're not like us? "Next stop, Overdrive. Overdrive . . ."

Gary Gambler saw Top Prime Cut smile broadly at the

early death of Red Rick: a long shot bet paid off. Gary resolved to follow his lead . . .

Karl tripped and the tinman was upon him with terrible efficiency . . .

The shambling scavenger, picking through the garbage can, thinking over ways of merging, raping, salivated at the thought of the next skin . . .

"Boy Vic" was a code name. They had landed in the wastes, entered Manville separately to avoid detection. Something had gone wrong, and his codes had been taken away from him, enmeshed in the skins. Or maybe that was the plan after all. And when the timer went off, the one skin had somehow come back to him like a homing pigeon, starting the reintegration process.

And now he was his true self again, a restored being. He had never been human.

Boy Vic spoke the Annihilation Code, saying, "I have come to burn the autumnal city."

There was a roar of blue-white light, a column of energy going straight up, and Manville was obliterated.

ABOUT THE AUTHOR

Michael Andre-Driussi is mainly known for his genre-reference books on Gene Wolfe (*Lexicon Urthus; Gate of Horn, Book of Silk; The Wizard Knight Companion*), John Crowley (*Snake's-hands*, co-edited with Alice K. Turner), and Jack Vance (*Handbook of Vance Space*). But he also writes fiction, such that dozens of his stories have been published in domestic and international venues, subsequently gathered in such collections as *Doomsday and Other Tours, Fallout Stories*, and *The Jizmatic Trilogy.*